"Why?" Clary as[ked]
"Why you, of all men?"

Morgan smiled bitterly at her. "Why not? One of fate's little jokes, my lovely. And refusing to believe it won't make it go away. I spent months trying!"

"You want me to be your lover," she said angrily.

"That's inevitable," he said with cool arrogance, "but that won't be enough. I want all of you. All the intelligence and spirit and character, all of the warmth and the kindness— everything. All of it, just for me."

Horrified, she stared at him. Her body was racked with unfulfilled longing, and she felt the nagging bite of unsatisfied passion.

It terrified her. *He* terrified her. She knew exactly how the defenders of some great fortress must have felt when the walls they trusted proved useless. Naked and bereft, betrayed by an enemy within.

ROBYN DONALD, her husband and their two children make their home in the far north of New Zealand where they indulge their love for outdoor life in general and sailing in particular. She keeps a file of clippings, photographs and a diary that she confides, "is useful in my work as well as for settling family arguments!"

Books by Robyn Donald

HARLEQUIN PRESENTS

HARLEQUIN ROMANCE

Don't miss any of our special offers. Write to us at the following address for information on our newest releases.

Harlequin Reader Service
901 Fuhrmann Blvd., P.O. Box 1397, Buffalo, NY 14240
Canadian address: P.O. Box 603,
Fort Erie, Ont. L2A 5X3

ROBYN DONALD

a willing surrender

Harlequin Books

TORONTO • NEW YORK • LONDON
AMSTERDAM • PARIS • SYDNEY • HAMBURG
STOCKHOLM • ATHENS • TOKYO • MILAN

Harlequin Presents first edition May 1987
ISBN 0-373-10976-8

Original hardcover edition published in 1986
by Mills & Boon Limited

CHAPTER ONE

IT was his height which first caught Clary's eyes. That, and the way the cool English sun summoned flames from the tawny head held so confidently.

A sudden scatter of applause from the crowd dragged her attention away from the tall stranger. Her slim capable hands added to the polite clapping as a flushed little girl tried to persuade her pony to leave the ring with some dignity. Amanda was a perfectionist, so her failure to clear two of the jumps would set her fretting for days. She would not, however, be grateful for any open commiseration.

Clary's dark-blue gaze shifted from her oldest charge to scan the crowd. Mostly mothers, except for a few au pairs like herself holding the fort for those parents unable to be there, they all looked similar to Clary's antipodean eyes. Well-cut skirts and Husky jackets, headscarves tied against the nasty little wind amounted almost to a uniform. Even Mrs Crowe, Amanda's mother and Clary's employer, a supremely elegant woman, blended into the crowd.

Clary's roaming eyes found the older woman. With every appearance of pleasure she was greeting the stranger, smiling up into his dark, striking face with open appreciation.

The tawny head inclined; there was a flash of white as the man smiled in response and said something which made Ginny Crowe and the two women with her break into laughter. Leona Sedbury—*Lady* Sedbury—smoothed a possessive hand over his forearm, mutely stressing her position as his escort.

The soft lines of Clary's mouth hardened as she took in the physical attributes which had sent every woman within reach into a pleasurable little flutter. His lean body, perfectly poised, was a sensual lure in itself, but the face above it radiated a magnetism which was frightening. The features were almost classically perfect except for an arrogant beak of a nose and an uncompromising mouth. Until he smiled, and then ruthlessness was transmuted into a potent, blazing charm.

Clary swallowed, recognising the odd tightening of her nerves. One did not reach the age of twenty-five without experiencing attraction, that primitive call of one sex to the other which signalled virility and the ability to impregnate. It was stupid to be so shaken by a blind natural force based only on the need to reproduce the species, but when the man smiled cool sensuality had crackled into vivid life.

Clary had good reason to distrust that sudden flare of excitement. In instinctive, involuntary defiance she straightened her shoulders, her expression altering into controlled indifference.

Perhaps it was the sudden movement, perhaps the smooth sheen of sunlight on the soft bronze waves of her hair which caught his attention. Eyes which were a strange mixture of gold and green lanced across the intervening space, assessed her coolly and comprehensively. Clary suffered the scrutiny of those eyes, almost wincing as they took in the measure of her face from the winged brows to the cleft chin which she and her brother had inherited from their father. The stranger's gaze probed the soft contours of her mouth, the wavy cap of hair and the scatter of freckles across her straight nose, the long lovely line of throat and neck.

No emotion disturbed the strong beauty of his face; it could have been a bronze mask turned towards her, yet Clary shivered, suddenly afraid. She sensed a response to the wildfire which ate through her body. For long moments they stared at each other across air which was as charged with energy as an electrical field.

A quick flame of colour scorched across her cheekbones, the pale skin revealing too blatantly the swift rise of blood beneath it. Astounded, she watched as an answering wash of colour smouldered beneath his bone-deep tan. It was as though that sudden attraction was some incandescent element, dangerous and beautiful as fire.

Across the heated, shimmering distance between them his eyes sent a message with all the impact of a laser.

Clary stiffened. The brutal, honest admission of desire produced such brazen arousal in her body that it was revealed only too plainly in her resentful eyes as they were held pinned by his. He was intent on staking some claim, imprinting her with the glamour of his lean face and the swift feral grace of a body perfectly proportioned, perfectly balanced.

Yet even while she exerted the willpower to turn away it was with the knowledge that when she remembered him it would be the stark power of the man she would recall, not his physical beauty.

Fortunately her bewildered glance fell upon a disconsolate little figure in jodhpurs wending its way towards her through the crowd. Almost dizzy with relief Clary scooped up the younger Crowe, who had been bouncing impetuously in her pushchair.

'Come on, darling,' Clary said, 'let's go and meet Amanda.'

Holding Beth like a shield she took the few steps necessary to reach Amanda, who, like all true horse-lovers, immediately began telling her how badly she had let down her pony.

She was still in full spate when her mother joined them a few minutes later.

'Well, it's over now,' Ginny intervened briskly. 'Everyone has trouble at first, don't they, Clary?'

Fixed by her minatory eye Clary smiled. 'Never having jumped I wouldn't know, but the first time you tackle anything you make mistakes. That's how you learn.'

Mrs Crowe nodded as Amanda's upturned face lost its woebegone look. 'Clary's right, of course, even if she doesn't ride. Somehow one always assumes that every New Zealander grows up in the saddle, but you're a city girl, aren't you?'

'I am. New Zealand's biggest city, at that. A tiddler by the rest of the world's standards, but it's the nearest thing to a metropolis we've got.'

'It doesn't appear to be big enough to keep Morgan Caird occupied.' Mrs Crowe nodded towards the bold stranger who now stood on the opposite side of the ring with Lady Sedbury and her husband, the owner of the local manor house. 'Mind you, he's more like a force of nature than a man, which probably explains why he has interests all over the world.'

'He's from Auckland?'

'Yes. His grandfather and Sedbury's were brothers.' Which, her tone revealed, made him *one of us*, acceptable.

Clary hid her astonishment with a smile, fascinated as always by the ramifications of a social system she barely understood even after three years spent mainly in the United Kingdom.

Ginny caught her amusement and laughed, saying, 'Oh, you colonials! You always manage to look smug as well as puzzled when you catch us being snobs. I refuse to believe that you don't have some sort of class system in your antipodean paradise.'

'Of course we do.' Clary's response was equally light. 'It's not nearly so rigid, though.'

Mrs Crowe's slender shoulders lifted in a little shrug. 'Oh well, it's all good clean fun. I should have thought that Morgan Caird would be known to you, he's quite famous even here—and not just for his looks.'

'An actor?'

'Hardly.' Mrs Crowe reacted to the waspish little suggestion with faint surprise. Her eyes were perceptive as they rested on Clary's disciplined features. 'I believe he's what is known as an entrepreneur.'

Clary's gaze skimmed the baby's hair to arrive at the tawny head poised so arrogantly above broad shoulders. 'Really?'

'Really. Don't you approve of entrepreneurs? Have I discovered a chink in that egalitarian armour you New Zealanders wear so righteously?'

'Never met one,' Clary told her cheerfully. 'Don't they go around buying up businesses and sacking old retainers? Asset-stripping, or some such thing?' Clary was deliberately vague, deliberately flippant, hoping that her employer would take her words to mean that she disliked the man instead of being unbearably attracted to him.

'I think it's a lot more technical than that,' Ginny said drily. 'Something like bringing together money and ideas and expertise. Whatever, Morgan Caird is a very clever man who has done exceptionally well for himself.'

'I believe you.' He certainly possessed that glittering air of success, that total assurance which came perilously close to arrogance.

'A fascinating creature. Leona Sedbury wanted him to stay longer than just one night but he put her off. She made a teasing comment about the woman he has left in London; apparently she's a stunning creature but she doesn't like the country. Anyway, Leona stupidly said something about it being a pity, and got a polite but very definite snub for her pains. Leona is a silly woman but she got the message.'

It was unlike Ginny Crowe to gossip and she didn't wait for any response, turning away immediately to ask Amanda about the rider then in the ring. Altogether too percipient, Clary decided wryly as she shifted little Beth from one hip to the other, smiling tenderly at the tired, rosy baby face. Somehow Ginny had divined that wild reaction in her au pair and had delivered her warning. Morgan Caird was not free.

Well, in the pleasant routine of her life with the Crowes Clary would soon forget that he had looked at her with naked desire and that her own sexuality had flamed up to meet it. It had happened before, it would happen again, that strange fever in the blood which some called chemistry and some desire. Clary called it lust, and despised it. At too early an age she had seen the havoc it made of people's lives, the ruin that the careless satisfaction of that most primal of urges brought in its wake, and she had no intention of allowing her pleasant life to be turned upside down by it.

I'll never see him again, she told herself very firmly.

Still, she was not altogether surprised later in the afternoon when Ginny appeared, her face totally without expression as she said, 'Leona Sedbury has just rung to ask if you would like to come with us to her party tonight. It's all very impromptu, very casual.'

It was nursery tea-time. Beth opened her mouth and after a moment Clary popped the spoon into it, coldly angry because her hand was shaking.

'I hope that you told her I was needed as a baby-sitter,' she said shortly.

'No, I said that I was sure you would like to come. Mrs Withers is quite happy to look after the children and it will be nice for you to meet someone from home, even if you don't like him much.'

Looking up sharply Clary met her employer's amused glance with a wry expression. 'You're very kind,' she said slowly, 'and probably right.'

'I often am. I shouldn't worry about Leona's manners, either. She's quite impartial about those she offends. Just put on a pretty dress—that coppery one would be very suitable—and enjoy yourself. You'll know most of the people there.'

Well, yes, but not socially. However Clary was curious as well as cautious and a party at Chase would give her something to write about in her next letter home. So she nodded and agreed, her mind going to the letter which had been delivered that morning. It was a strangely unsatisfying communication in spite of the breezy chattiness which was her mother's epistolary style. If she hadn't known her better Clary would have assumed that life at home was going on its usual pleasant way, but she could remember other letters disturbingly similar to this one, too cheerful to be true. Letters written to hide a broken heart; letters from a woman whose husband had left her for a much younger lover. Helen Grey had developed that particular style to hide the truth so that Clary could sit her University Entrance examinations without added stress.

As always whenever she thought of her father Clary's expression hardened into a frightening severity, until little Beth's whimper forced a smile and a remorseful cuddle.

'It was a long time ago,' she said gently, almost as if to reassure herself, 'and it's all over now. But oh, I wish I knew what's bothering my mama.'

Not that there was anything she could do about it. The twelve thousand miles which lay between them might just as well be infinity for all that she could do to bridge them. Suddenly angry with herself for having promised to stay with the Crowes another five months, she was consoled by the fact that whatever worried her mother she had Angus and Susan to support her through it.

Angus was so utterly dependable, bless him. He had been the perfect older brother, a little reserved perhaps, but completely reliable, as strong as a rock.

His wife was pleasant, although she too was reserved; Clary had met her a year ago when they had flown across to London for their honeymoon. She would have chosen someone warmer, more spontaneous and outgoing for Angus, but he had obviously been completely bowled over by his wife's fragile beauty, and Clary knew that the paths of the heart are not always easily understood. As always when she thought of Susan, Clary crossed her fingers in foreboding. Then she laughed and gave Beth another hug, saying cheerfully, 'All gone, my little bird. No more.'

Beth gave her an enchanting gummy smile and clapped her hands before holding out imperious arms.

'OK.' Clary released the highchair catch. 'Come on, honeybun, time for your bath, and then cuddles with Mummy, and then, chickadee, bed!'

The copper dress did suit her, Clary decided as she finished her toilet by spraying some of her precious 'First' perfume on her throat and wrists. The glowing copper lent warmth to her pale skin and the silky material swathed her body with loving precision, but it was subdued in design so she wouldn't stand out; with any luck she could spend a pleasant evening inconspicuously watching the county enjoy itself. If she did get to meet the guest of honour—well, they could discuss such peculiarly New Zealand things as sheep, and Rugby, and mountain-climbing . . .

Unfortunately for her decision to blend with the wallpaper Lady Sedbury greeted her as if she were a long-lost bosom friend and introduced her to Morgan Caird with the sly little declaration, 'Morgan is *very* anxious to meet you, Clary. He described you so graphically that I knew immediately who you were.' Her glance lingered on Clary's high full breasts, and the long line from hip to ankle with enough meaning to bring the angry colour to her victim's cheeks.

Clary lifted goaded eyes to Morgan's handsome face

but saw nothing there except an aloof appreciation. However bold his appraisal that afternoon, he was giving nothing away now, parrying his hostess's poisonous little dart with an impersonal courtesy which cooled Clary's anger.

Like well-trained actors the Crowes and he defused the situation with the kind of effortless good manners which should have made Leona Sedbury ashamed. It didn't. When the Crowes moved on, taking a thankful Clary with them, it was with the memory of malice in Lady Sedbury's smile and sleepy blue eyes.

However the first part of the evening was enjoyable enough. That same relentless courtesy ensured that no one evinced any surprise at the sudden social elevation of the Crowes' au pair, and after a while she found herself in cheerful conversation with a young married couple. They had relations in New Zealand and were thinking of going there for a holiday, so they were eager for information.

Clary obliged, trying hard not to allow her homesickness too free a rein, and thought she was doing rather well until she noticed that she had lost the woman's attention entirely. Sudden awareness widened the eyes which had been fixed on Clary's face; they looked past her now and one hand moved automatically to touch an errant lock, lingering there in a gesture as unconscious as it was provocative.

The deep crisp voice with its faint New Zealand accent fell painfully on Clary's ear as Morgan Caird greeted them by name. Good memory, she decided and stood without looking his way while he charmed both husband and wife. No doubt an entrepreneur would need an excellent memory. The charm would come in handy, too.

He had other skills as well, probably equally useful. She wasn't in the least surprised when after a short time she found herself alone with him, separated from everyone else by an exquisite screen; in fact, she almost admired the adroitness with which he disentangled them from the English couple.

'Superbly done,' she said. 'I'll bet you have no trouble in your boardrooms.'

He grinned down at her, appreciating the sarcasm. 'Very little I can't handle. Now, what part of New Zealand do you come from?'

The usual question, asked by all expatriates, however temporary. 'Auckland,' she told him remotely, concentrating very hard on the beautiful colours and textures of the silk screen. 'However, I haven't been there for some years.'

'Getting your overseas experience?'

Her shoulders lifted slightly, dismissively. 'Yes.'

Half of one of those years had been spent nursing in a refugee camp in the Far East, but he wouldn't be interested in that. Refugees, with their almost insurmountable problems, tended to embarrass most people. They felt guilty because there was so little they could do; they didn't want to hear about children who starved or died of unpronounceable diseases.

'When do you go back home?'

Another small shrug. Still without looking at him she said, 'In the autumn. I promised my employers I'd stay until the baby is a year old.'

'When you picked her up today I thought she was yours.'

Something in the deep tones impelled Clary's glance towards him. She fell an immediate captive to the strange glittering depths of his eyes. He looked tense, those perfect features too prominently emphasised as though the skin had tightened over them.

Hastily she renewed her scrutiny of the screen. A peculiar shortness of breath made her unusually hesitant. 'I'm surprised that you were so explicit in your description of me to Lady Sedbury. Or do you not care whether a woman is married or not?'

'Oh, I care,' he returned, quiet voice at variance

with the hard authority of his features. 'But nowadays
a child doesn't necessarily mean a marriage. Then
there was always the possibility that you were no
longer interested in its father.'

'Do you do this often?' she asked with totally
spurious interest. 'I mean, I believe you're only going
to be here one night. I've also been told that you have
a girlfriend waiting for you in London. Can't you
spend even one night alone?'

The directness of her attack astounded her but she
refused to back down; instead her chin lifted a fraction
as she met his hard, bright glare.

His anger was clear. The wide sensual mouth had
tightened into a thin line, the handsome face suddenly
invested with an implacable authority which probably
had sent whole boards of directors cowering. Well, not
me, Clary thought with defiance.

And then the harshness dissolved into amusement
accompanied by an open, bold appraisal which made
her conscious of heat building in the pit of her
stomach.

'All that because I was crass enough to describe you
to Leona as well-endowed,' he said with smooth
mockery. 'I'm sorry. I also told her that you had hair
the colour of new gum leaves, and a curly, very
kissable mouth, that you were just the right height for
a man as tall as I am, and that the cleft in your chin
gives you an air of enchanting wilfulness.' A long sun-
browned finger detailed the cleft with a lover's touch
before moving to outline the sweep of jaw and the coil
of her ear.

Bewildered by the sudden rush of sensations which
held her in thrall, Clary blinked. Her throat was too
tight to allow any sound to escape; that warmth which
had begun in her stomach washed through the rest of
her body. Her last ounce of common sense told her
that she must look a perfect fool, staring mesmerised
into his face while he smiled down at her with the

masterful assurance of a man who knew he could break hearts.

Hoarsely she muttered, 'I'll bet you didn't tell her all that, either.'

'I may have missed out a few adjectives.' He moved closer, broad shoulders shutting out the room and the people behind him. 'I didn't tell her that your eyes are the colour of the sheen on a tui's wing, or that there are eight freckles on that arrogant little nose, either. But I knew. And that your legs are long and slim and shapely, or that your waist is excitingly curved beneath those lovely breasts. I also didn't tell her that I've discovered in myself a quite startling ability to fantasise, and that, in the short time between the moment I first saw you and now, I've already overworked it! I daresay Leona would have understood, but she has this unfortunate habit of blurting out the truth at the most awkward moments. Besides, I wanted to tell you myself.'

Oh God, Clary thought desperately as his finger stroked across her full bottom lip then moved up her cheek to trace the high winging flare of a brow. This had never happened before, this overwhelming abandonment to sensation. Secure behind the walls of her contempt for those who couldn't control their sexuality, she had always been able to subdue the inconvenient manifestations of desire.

Was this glowing flood of heat and fire what had dragged her father from his wife's arms? Clary's scorn, and the contempt she had felt for her father since his love affair with a woman twenty years younger than he, were replaced by a bitter comprehension. At that moment Morgan Caird dominated her completely. The cool logic which usually characterised her thought processes was gone, swept away by a primitive, animal need. All that was feminine—all that was *female*—in her called to be taken by his male strength, possessed and used and impregnated.

And then cast aside, she thought savagely, noting the glitter of triumph in the narrowed eyes, the hint of satisfaction in the curve of that disciplined mouth.

Stepping back she said harshly, 'Very pretty, Mr Caird. Unfortunately I'm not in the mood for ravishment by poetic phrases tonight.'

She expected him to be angry. At the very least he should have been irritated by her rejection.

But the infuriating man smiled almost sympathetically, as though he understood her panic, and took her hand and said, 'Then let's see if I can seduce you with the perfection of my dancing!'

She tried to jerk free but he was ready for such an obvious manoeuvre. As his fingers tightened she exclaimed, 'Ouch.'

'Sorry, did I hurt?'

He wasn't sorry, and he knew that he hadn't hurt her. That grip was his far-from-subtle way of asserting control as he guided her towards the room where music was projecting an insistent, potent lure. She was too tense to notice the covert glances they were getting from many of the guests. And when, in the dimly lit room, he turned her into his arms, she admitted to herself that she was really frightened.

Of course he danced well. That perfectly balanced athlete's body probably did everything well. Including making love. A hot shiver quickened her shallow breathing as a sudden image of him bending over her, of her flung wantonly across a great bed, was followed by even more explicit imagery, the contrast between her pale fine skin and the dark shading of his, his strength and her comparative weakness——

Oh God! she thought, pornography! In my own brain! Stiffly she pulled away from the body her own craved.

It was a tactical mistake. Until then he had been holding her fairly loosely but now his arm tightened and she was pulled into such close proximity that his

jaw brushed her forehead, the texture of his skin allied
to the strength of the frame beneath it making her
angrily aware of her capacity for eroticism. With
savage enjoyment she heard the sudden harsh breath
he gave, felt the moment when every muscle in his
lithe frame locked into rigidity.

'When are you going back home?' Yes, that was her
voice, so heavily regimented that it was expressionless.

'A fortnight from now.' He bent his head so that the
answer was almost whispered into her ear. His breath
was warm, sensuously activating nerves she had never
before known she possessed.

Taunted by his faint male fragrance she rested her
forehead against his neck.

'Come up to London with me,' he said thickly, the
words seemingly jerked from him without volition.

So this was temptation! Intuition told her that his
proposition was totally out of character. It would be
just as uncharacteristic of her to agree.

But oh, how to refuse when every nerve and cell in
her body begged for fulfilment?

'What about the girlfriend?' she asked at last in an
icily remote little voice.

'Oh God, she's not important. Nothing matters any
longer—but this.' He had guided them into another
secluded corner—later, when she recovered her sanity
Clary would realise that such expertise in discovering
these corners bespoke considerable experience—and as
he spoke his hand swooped down past her waist and
for a long moment her hips were forced against his and
she was left in no doubt as to his arousal.

Although she could not have prevented him he did
not attempt to kiss her, but his gaze burned across her
throbbing mouth. The clamour of her senses silenced
her. It was the most erotic experience of her life, yet to
onlookers it must have seemed as though they did
nothing more than dance, for they were still swaying
in time to the music.

'Stay with me,' he said between his teeth. 'Come back to New Zealand with me.'

She shuddered with longing, but shook her head.

'Please,' he whispered. 'Please, Clary, I need you.'

'You know I can't.' But her hand stole up to curve into the side of his face, her sensitive fingers feeling the life impulse at the austere temple, her palm over the sharply defined cheekbone, the heel of her hand sensitised to the muscles clenched along the strong jaw. Gold-green eyes blazed into hers, willing her, compelling her to surrender.

'I only know that this has never happened to me before.' The warm strength of his hand held hers in place as he turned his face into her palm, kissing it with a driving passion which had no place for subtlety. 'I looked at you and it was like being spun out of this time, this dimension, into one where the old romantic values hold true. Love at first sight, the princess in the tower, the enchantress who can snare a man's heart from his body... My God, if you'd been married I was going to seduce you away from your husband, and I have never had anything but contempt for men who sleep with married women! I must have you, but you terrify me...'

The thick, impeded declaration faded, as though he dared not face the implications of what he was saying. Shaken by the ferocious intensity she glimpsed in his face Clary fought fiercely to contain the whirlwind of response which raged within her.

'Then leave me alone,' she managed to whisper after a false start. 'I don't want this. I can't go with you, I have responsibilities here. And you have a responsibility to the woman who's waiting for you in London.'

He muttered something short and explicit beneath his breath then pushed her away. 'I won't let you escape so easily,' he said tonelessly, reasserting control over his emotions with an effort which showed. 'I can't dance any more with you, but there are other things we can do to fill in time. I want to know you, and not only in the Biblical sense.'

Heat scorched up her cheeks, ached through her body. On legs which felt as though someone had removed the bones, she walked with him into the room where those who didn't want to dance were occupying themselves with talk and flirtation.

I must be mad, she thought bitterly. Frustrated and ready for a fling with the first personable male who has shown an interest in me for a time.

'Relax,' he said, all the passion of a few minutes ago hidden by a sardonic smile. 'You look as though someone had punched you in the stomach.'

She managed to produce an answering smile, taking comfort that in this crowd it should be easy enough to lose him. So she greeted their host with equanimity, gracefully accepted his heavy-handed compliments and waited for an opportunity to get away.

Plenty came her way, but she got nowhere. From beneath hooded eyes Morgan watched and kept her right beside him, either physically with an arm across her shoulders or by making her such an integral part of the conversation that she could not slip away without being rude. By nature an observer rather than a participator she found it a strain, almost as much as an evening spent fighting off his advances would have been. When at last the Crowes came over she greeted them with a smile which beseeched help.

'We're on our way,' Ginny said, her shrewd eyes amused yet oddly sympathetic.

'I'm ready to go.' Clary mixed just the right blend of tiredness and regret into the words as she moved to separate herself from Morgan.

But no one outmanoeuvred Morgan Caird. He came to the car with them, and before putting Clary into the back seat he claimed both her hands, kissing one then the other, the backs first followed by a slow sensuous

caress of both palms, folding her fingers over to keep
the kisses intact.

'Until we see each other again,' he said, mockery
almost hiding an undertone of raw emotion.

Very inadequately Clary said, 'Goodbye,' and
almost fell into the car, scrubbing her hands against
her thighs to rid herself of his touch.

From the front Ginny's laughter grated on her
nerves. 'What style,' she exclaimed. 'My God, the
man has everything!'

Except integrity. Bitterness stung Clary's throat and
eyes. Freed at last from the spell of that overwhelming
masculinity she was able to appreciate clearly just
what sort of swine he was. *I must have you*, he had
said, so intent on his own selfish desire that he didn't
consider hers at all!

Thank heavens he was going back to London the
next day.

She spent the night trying extremely hard to sleep,
and failing. It was with enormous gratitude that she
watched the sky lighten and heard Beth's early-
morning whimper.

Routine was soothing, inducing in her enough
composure to banish both her memories of the night
before and the shameful fantasies which she had not
been able to control in the sleepless hours in her bed.
Unfortunately her calmness was shattered when the
daily came in, looking interested and speculative.

'It's a man on the phone for you, dear,' she said,
smiling. 'Sounds ever so like you.'

Clary set down her coffee-cup. Subconsciously she
had known that he would contact her before he left
Chase; with a stern expression she picked up the receiver.

'Clary? How did you sleep?'

'Like the dead,' she said.

His laughter was soft and knowing. 'Liar! I couldn't
either. That over-active imagination of mine kept me
awake. When can I see you?'

'You can't,' she said baldly. 'I mean it, Morgan. I don't want anything to do with you.'

'Well, that's a pity,' he observed, all humour banished from the deep voice so that it sounded flatly relentless. 'Why?'

'Because you frighten me,' she blurted.

That made him laugh, although there was no amusement in the sound. 'I frighten myself,' he told her. 'And you scare the hell out of me, but the only way to cure fear is to face it. So when am I going to see you next? I know you have this coming weekend——'

'No. Not then, not ever. *Never*. I don't want to have anything to do with you—with the sort of man you are.'

'And what sort of man is that?' he asked with silky clarity.

Clary shivered but went ahead just the same, venting her fear and frustration into the cutting words. 'The sort of man who propositions one woman while still entangled with another. And trying to convince me that she isn't important is not going to advance your cause any, either.'

'Clary.'

Just her name, spoken without emotion, yet she couldn't hang up. Her fingers ached with tension but the receiver stayed pressed to her ear.

'Clary,' he said again and this time she bit her lip at the implacable purpose in his voice. 'I won't let it end like this. Whatever there is between us is something I have never known before and I want to experience it fully. If I have to I'll hunt you down. Don't make me.'

Her teeth bit into her lip until the pain made her wince. 'Don't think you can threaten me into your bed,' she said thinly.

'Threaten, force, bribe, blackmail—I don't care how I do it. I want you,' he said tonelessly. 'I'd prefer to persuade, though. Clary——'

'No!'

This time she managed to cut the connection, slamming the receiver down viciously.

Back in the kitchen she said to Mrs Withers, 'If anyone else rings please tell them I'm not at home. I'm taking the baby for her vaccination now.'

'And if he calls in, dear?'

'Tell him you don't know where I am. Please.'

'Well, you know your business best, I suppose. All right, I'll tell him.'

Mrs Crowe had gone up to London for the day leaving Clary with the small car. Expecting any minute to see Morgan appear she popped Beth and a bag of necessities into it and left in a hurry. Just as if he were an ogre, she thought, trying for her normal sense of humour. Not that he looked like an ogre; she frowned fiercely, trying to banish his image from her mind. But it stayed all the time she waited patiently for Beth's vaccination and even as she comforted the indignant baby she could still see the lithe graceful body, the slashing beauty of his features and that worldly mouth.

'Darling, darling, do hush,' she whispered into the soft, baby-smelling hair. 'Come on, poppet, time to get you home. Do stop crying!'

By the time they arrived back the daily had gone but she had left an envelope propped up against the kettle. Clary didn't need to read the little note written on the back of it to know who had left it. *He came!!! You're mad!!* Mrs Withers had written.

After Beth had had her lunch and gone grumpily to bed Clary made herself a cup of tea. Only when it was poured did she slit the envelope and unfold the paper inside.

Clary, he wrote, *I meant what I said. I'd much rather you came willingly to me, but if I have to I will find you if it means tearing the world apart. Last night I begged. Next time I might just take.* It finished with an address—at the Connaught Hotel—and a telephone number.

'Charming,' Clary said contemptuously, crumpling the paper before throwing it into the rubbish.

He was nothing but a conceited, big-headed flirt, making threats he must know he couldn't carry out. Her rejection had hurt his pride and he didn't know how to cope with it. But she couldn't help remembering the desperation with which he had pleaded with her to go with him. Until then he had appeared vastly self-possessed, with a pride and disciplined arrogance that was intimidating. It seemed incredible that such a man should have surrendered to the wild urgings of a physical attraction, however intense.

CHAPTER TWO

THE Crowes said nothing to her about Morgan Caird, for which Clary was thankful. She was having enough difficulty prising him out of her brain without any reinforcement from outside.

So it was with a sinking heart that she met Lady Sedbury outside the village shop a few days later. She had to stiffen her sinews to meet the narrow smile with which she was greeted, and the faint flash of malice which seemed ever-present in the older woman's expression.

'And what you been buying, Amanda?'

'It's Clary's birthday present,' Amanda told her importantly. 'She's going to be twenty-five next Saturday.'

'Ah, what it is to be twenty-five! How is this momentous occasion to be celebrated?'

'Clary is going to London. She is going out to dinner with friends, but they haven't chosen the restaurant yet. Clary doesn't know very many restaurants in London.'

Lady Sedbury's rather feline smile was reflected in her long blue eyes. 'Adrian's is an excellent place to dine,' she observed. 'It's not madly expensive and the food is divine.'

'Adrian's,' Ginny observed when Amanda reported the little exchange. 'Yes, you'd almost certainly enjoy it, Clary. It has an English menu—good regional dishes and superb salmon and venison. You could do a lot worse.'

So Clary rang Donna Evans, who was organising the London end of things. 'Oh, *yes*!' said Donna enthusiastically. 'I read a review which raved about their steak and kidney pudding. I'll make reservations today.' Donna adored steak and kidney pudding.

On Saturday morning Clary was driven to the station by her employer who waved her off with strict injunctions to enjoy herself. Until the train was out of sight Clary waved the handkerchief decorated with horseshoes which was Amanda's present, then settled back into the seat, pleasantly cheered by the anticipation of two whole days of freedom.

There had been a parcel from New Zealand, from her mother, and a card from Angus with a cheque in it; before settling down with the biography which her employers had given her Clary wondered at that card. The message in it was affectionate enough but there was no indication that Susan had had anything to do with it; she had not signed it and Angus had not included her, and that was unusual.

'Oh, don't go looking for trouble,' she adjured herself sternly as she opened the biography, hoping rather fervently that it would keep her mind off the fact that Morgan Caird was in London. She was becoming quite good at banishing him from her mind although the prickling unease his name sent through her was a little harder to dismiss. Still, by blocking out that evening, by refusing to recall any of it, she was overcoming the weakness of a brain and body which were too easily traitors.

Donna was waiting, her brilliant curls lighting up the drab, busy station. 'You've lost weight, you louse!' she exclaimed, hugging Clary with her usual enthusiasm. 'Don't you dare think of dieting for the next forty-eight hours. We are going to enjoy ourselves!'

Which they did, with the help of Donna's vibrant personality and the Victoria and Albert museum and Clary's determination to put away the unease which niggled at her, at least for this weekend.

Back at the flat which Donna shared with three other girls, two away for the weekend and one incommunicado in a bedroom, they drank coffee, caught up on news from home, and got ready.

'I thought I saw Angus's wife the other day,' Donna called from the bathroom as she applied her mascara. 'In Harrod's, but I couldn't get a close look at her. It was as crowded as usual. Same gorgeous fall of red hair, though. Whoever it was was in the designer room.'

'Not Susan. Angus hasn't made his fortune yet.'

Clary smoothed her dress down over her hips. It looked good, the rich blue fabric clinging caressingly. Another timeless design, the long full sleeves and shirt collar suited her height and the narrow belt emphasised her slim waist. She used a smoky violet to shadow her eyes and a slight smoothing of blusher because the blue tended to make her pale skin look even paler.

'Ravishing,' Donna pronounced, vivid as a fire-cracker in yellow and gold which she wore with the panache and flair that was an integral part of her character. 'Ah, this sounds like the boys.'

The boys were both English, brothers, the older of whom, James Preston, was Donna's boyfriend. His brother John was, like him, tall and thin and pleasant. Clary had met them before and liked them.

The restaurant was warm and gracious, with a head waiter who combined authority with an air of benevolence which caused Donna to compare him to Mr Pickwick. The service was good, too. The first drinks came quickly, and they were left to peruse the menu in peace; apparently Adrian's did not believe in hovering unnecessarily. All in all, Clary decided as she sipped her sherry, it had the makings of a very enjoyable dinner.

It continued to be a good evening until just before it finished. Donna was slowly absorbing a superb summer pudding when she looked over John's shoulder and exclaimed, 'Clary, isn't that your— Clary!'

For Clary had seen too, and her face was as white as the cloth beneath her plate.

'No, don't go, you can't make a scene . . .'

But Clary was already on her feet, her eyes enormous in her face as she watched Morgan Caird and his companion being ushered to their table.

'Oh my God! Oh, *stop* her!' Donna moaned, but it was too late.

Moving stiffly like an automaton Clary made her way across the room. She was terrified, her whole body clenched in a bitter amalgam of pain and anger, yet nothing could have stopped her as she walked between the tables, oblivious to the low murmur of interest which followed her. A pace away from the table the two occupants saw her. Morgan got to his feet, his face carved from stone, but Clary ignored him completely.

'Hello, Susan,' she said to the beautiful red-headed woman who was staring at her as if she had appeared from hell. 'Where is Angus?'

And watched with cold cruel eyes as her sister-in-law's lashes fell in shamed confusion.

'Sit down.' Morgan's voice was soft but uncompromising, as were the fingers which fastened on to her arm and urged her down into a chair.

'Where is Angus?' she repeated mercilessly.

Susan's tongue touched her lips. She sent a desperate glance to Morgan and he said, 'Susan has left him. Clary——'

'To be your mistress? The one you told me twice was of no importance?' Her voice cracked on a laugh. 'That was when he was trying to talk me into taking your place, Susan. Or joining you, I'm not sure which.'

'You'd better have something to drink,' Morgan said, his expression impassive. A waiter appeared, and a moment later, two brandies.

Susan drank hers quickly, shivering, her eyes avoiding Clary, but Clary shook her head.

'I've already had enough,' she said coldly. 'If I have
any more I might get maudlin. You'd have a worse
scene on your hands then.' She stared at Morgan with
open contempt. 'I'm not sure that even your practised
sophistication could deal with that.'

'Try me and see,' he invited grimly.

She considered this for some moments. Perhaps it
was the wine she had drunk with her meal which gave
her such an odd disconnected feeling. Beneath the
outward calm there was a freezing, savagely vindictive
rage which could not be unleashed, or she just might
kill them both.

'When did you leave Angus?' she asked politely,
turning her blank eyes to her sister-in-law.

Again Susan shot a terrified glance towards Morgan
but Clary intervened, 'Answer me yourself, please.'

'A—a month ago.'

Clary nodded almost judicially. 'About the time my
mother's letters became evasive. Have you left him for
good, or do you plan to go back after this little fling?'

'Clary, for God's sake——'

'But I want to know, Susan.'

Susan gave a long shuddering sigh. 'I've left him for
good.'

'Then I hope that you have extracted quite a lot of
money from your lover,' Clary said without com-
punction, 'because I don't think your tenure is exactly
secure.'

'That will do!' Morgan did not raise his voice but it
cracked like a whip. As Susan's lips trembled he
reached over to cover her shaking hands in a
protective gesture which cut through Clary like the
bitterest of betrayals. 'If you want to hurt anyone,' he
said, staring at Clary, 'try me. It won't be quite as
much fun because I'm a lot tougher than Susan, but
you are welcome to use me as a whipping-post. If you
are prepared to take the consequences.'

She smiled with fierce irony. 'Could anything hurt

you? Monumental conceit like yours is armour against anything the world can throw your way, isn't it? Why shouldn't Susan suffer a little? I don't suppose Angus is feeling overly cheerful at the moment, and I can guarantee he isn't eating in a place like this with a woman as accommodating as she is.'

She rose, meeting Morgan's compelling, controlled anger with a faint cold smile. Both ignored Susan's imploring repetition of her name. Darkest-blue eyes flamed into green-gold ones. 'I hope you enjoy yourselves as much as I have,' she finished, turning to nod at the couple who arrived beside them. 'Lady Sedbury, Lord Sedbury,' she said tonelessly before walking back across the room.

'We're ready to go,' Donna told her quietly. Clearly she had filled in some of the details to the men, who looked both shifty and protective, as men anticipating a scene do. 'Hold your head high and smile. John, take her arm without beng too obvious.'

They were kind, and they shielded her from the too-interested eyes of the rest of the diners, and Clary was more grateful than she could ever express. Once in the car long shudders racked her body; she had to clench her teeth and her hands to prevent the tears from coming.

At the flat Donna dismissed the men, forced a large brandy down her throat then dealt kindly and competently with the bout of weeping which followed, holding Clary in maternal arms until she had cried herself to a standstill.

'You'll feel better if you wash your face,' she advised. 'Get into your nightdress and I'll make some tea. Do you have a headache?'

'Yes, but it will go. I don't need a pain-killer.'

The tea was fragrant and faintly lemon-flavoured, exactly as Clary liked it. Together they drank it in silence, until Donna said, 'I suppose you had to find out some time, but what filthy luck that they had to choose that restaurant!'

By now the pounding in Clary's head had receded. She looked across at Donna's sympathetic face and gave an odd little grimace. 'That wasn't luck.' Briefly she explained Lady Sedbury's part in the choosing of Adrian's.

'But she didn't know Susan. I don't understand . . .'

'She knew that Morgan Caird would be there. With Susan. With his mistress.'

'But—oh. *Oh*, I see! Oh, for heaven's sake. Where did you meet him? Down there? I see, I wondered why you were so intense. Honestly, you scared the living daylights out of me. Susan, too. She really did seem to shrink. You looked like everybody's image of an avenging angel, I kept looking for the fiery sword. Shut me up, I'm gabbling.'

Clary's eyes filled with tears. She drained the rest of her tea then blew her nose. Looping her hands around her knees she said quietly, 'It was just an unhappy coincidence that Morgan Caird's lover happened to be my sister-in-law.'

'Morgan Caird!' Donna set her cup down. 'He's well named.'

Clary looked her surprise and Donna elaborated, 'Henry Morgan was a pirate on the Spanish Main. If I remember correctly he turned respectable after a lifetime of wickedness. Morgan Caird looks as if he'd have enjoyed being a pirate and I shouldn't think there's a respectable bone in that superb body. How hard did you fall, Clary?'

'Well, I didn't go to bed with him.' She told Donna as much as she felt necessary for her to know, downplaying that searing attraction in a monotonous recital of facts.

'Why on earth should her ladyship want to upset you? Or embarrass you? She sounds a right bitch.'

'I think—from things I've heard—that she likes little flirtations. Nothing serious, just fun. I suppose she thought that Morgan might join her in her games. Perhaps she was piqued when he didn't. I don't know, perhaps she saw a chance to punish us a little. If I hadn't taken her suggestion about Adrian's, well, she'd have lost nothing. She wouldn't have known that Susan was my brother's wife. That was the filthy luck. I'm so sorry I spoiled the evening.'

Donna said something brief and explicit which brought a smile to Clary's pale lips. Suddenly immensely weary, she was purged now of all emotion but her anguish for her brother. Angling her head against the back of the rather uncomfortable chair which was the best the flat had to offer, she said, 'Lord, but I made a fool of myself!'

'Hardly anyone noticed. You know Londoners, they wouldn't have bothered if you'd stripped naked in front of them! That's what I like about them.'

Silence, broken only by the swish of a late car heading home through the rain.

'Clary?'

'Mm?'

'What happened between you and Morgan Caird? It's not like you to lose your cool so completely over a man.'

The controlled curves of Clary's mouth twisted caustically. 'I believe it's known as lust at first sight,' she said. 'It was as if—as if my body took over. It was horrible—I felt so helpless.'

'And did he feel the same way?'

'He said so. I think—yes, he did.'

Another period of silence while Clary fought the acrid sense of betrayal which ate corrosively into her, fuelling a resurgence of the vitriolic anger she had suffered when she had seen Morgan's tawny head inclined towards Susan's, her long, beautifully manicured fingers so possessively resting on his arm. Then as now, Clary's whole being had cried out in bitter protest.

Without asking Donna poured them both another cup of tea. To take her mind off the torment which racked her Clary said dully, 'I'd better ring my mother. She'll tell me how Angus is.'

'Shattered, I suppose.'

'I'm afraid so. He worshipped Susan. The *bitch!*'

'He's better off without her,' Donna said with brisk common sense. 'It's a cliché, but it's true.'

Clary pushed a hand through her tumbled hair. 'My father died of a broken heart,' she said without emotion. 'When his lover left him he crawled back home like a beaten dog and withered away. He loved her to the point of obsession.'

'And you think Angus—oh, Clary, I'm sure you're wrong.' Donna was appalled. 'I've only met him a couple of times, but your brother struck me as being a very strong character with far too much personality to give up like your father, whatever the temptation.'

Clary closed her eyes. 'Oh, God, I hope so,' she whispered. 'If anything happens I swear I'll kill Susan. And Morgan Caird.'

'You're so tired you don't know what you're saying,' Donna told her, secretly more than worried at the pitiless determination which hardened Clary's face into an ancient, primitive mask. 'Come on, let's go to bed. Things always seem better in the morning.'

They did, but not much, and it was an exhausted Clary who spoke to her mother across twelve thousand miles, telling her nothing of Morgan Caird, only that she had seen Susan.

'I won't tell Angus that you met her,' Mrs Grey said after her first shocked exclamations. 'I honestly think that the less said of her the better.'

'How is he?'

There was a slight silence intensified by her mother's sigh. 'He's taking it very hard. He's working like a maniac at his job, and as far as I can tell he spends most of the night in his workshop. He hasn't said much, you know Angus. He's confident that this latest thing he's working on will come to something. It's something to do with navigation in aeroplanes.'

'At least he's got something to do,' Clary said softly, remembering the grey-faced man who had been her father as he sat waiting for death.

'Yes.' Mrs Grey's voice firmed, became positive. 'Now don't you go worrying your soul over this. Angus is a big boy now and he'll survive. I didn't rear weaklings!'

Clary managed to laugh. Her mother's matronly appearance belied the strong character which had kept her on an even keel through her husband's betrayal and enabled her to give him refuge free from recriminations when he had come back to her without prospects or hope.

'We are so looking forward to seeing you, Clary. Be happy.'

Clary hung up and turned to meet Donna's eyes. 'Well,' she said on a long exhalation of breath, 'that was a suitably expurgated version. She told me to be happy!'

'Why not?' Donna said robustly. 'I think most people are about as happy as they want to be.'

Which was easy enough to say; in the months which followed Clary found herself wondering why the situation should have the power to produce the kind of bitterness she found herself suffering. OK, she said to herself innumerable times, so you met a man who looked like an erotic fantasy and made you feel as though you were playing a central role in just that. That was all it had been, lust, passion, carnal love— only love was too kind a word to describe it. There had been no love in their reaction to each other. If she hadn't been so frightened at the primitive power of the emotion they would have coupled like animals, mating with total, sensual abandon until the flame died, as was inevitable, and then she would have despised herself for the rest of her life.

Gradually she managed to push the memories and the emotions they caused far enough into her subconscious to give some relief from the tension they brought, helped by both Crowe children who became increasingly dear to her.

About Angus their mother's letters were cautiously optimistic. He had obtained a separation order and now had only to wait out the two years for the divorce to be finalised. He was still working incredibly hard, but he had found a consortium who were definitely interested in backing his latest invention, which would be a marvellous boost for his morale. Angus made quite a good income from the patents on several of his gadgets but from what her mother wrote, this one was big-time.

Halfway through a bleak northern autumn Clary kissed Amanda and Beth goodbye, said her farewells to their parents and realised with quite intense relief that she would no longer have to see Lady Sedbury or parry her malicious little remarks. Several times the other woman had tried to get some reaction from Clary, mentioning the evening at Adrian's with delicate effrontery. Each time Clary had stared blankly at her, treating the impertinent enquiries with calm seriousness. In the end Leona had given up, but her appearance was a continual reminder to Clary of the worst evening of her life, and she was glad not to have to cope with it any more.

She made her farewells to the rest of the village with considerable regret and went on up to London with all her worldly goods in one suitcase and a pack.

She spent a hectic week getting ready for Donna's wedding to James Preston, at which she was bridesmaid. After that she shifted to a small bed-and-breakfast place and made final preparations for the flight back home. In between she indulged in last-minute sightseeing, trying to cram into a few days as many as she could of the sights she had previously missed. It was enjoyable being on her own; solitude suited her mood exactly.

The day before her plane left she was walking down the Haymarket on her way to the National Gallery when it began to rain, hard pelting drops which persuaded her into New Zealand House, where she decided to wait out the shower. There, reading a newspaper from Wellington, she met a girl with whom she had once spent a miserably wet weekend in a youth hostel in the Lake District.

After the usual surprised greetings the girl said, 'Did you know there's a note for you in the rack? It's been there a while.'

'No! I'd better check it out. Nice to see you again.'

'You too. Give my love to Enzed, won't you.'

Smiling, Clary promised to do that, then made her way to the rack which held the slightly creased envelope. The note was concise to the point of starkness. *Clary, please contact Susan*, it read, and was followed by a London telephone number.

It took an effort not to shred the paper. What prevented her was that after that last traumatic meeting she knew Susan would only try to contact her if it was vitally important.

Slowly, her jaw tightening painfully, she folded the note several times before thrusting it into her pocket. She went down the stairs and across the marble floor to the lower level which held the telephones.

It seemed an omen when one of the normally busy booths was free. Ignoring an extremely interested appraisal from the man next to her she dialled, heard Susan's voice and fatalistically pushed the coin home.

'It's Clary here. I've just got your note. Is anything wrong?'

'No.' The silence, short and tense, rang in her ears. Then Susan said, 'I'd almost given up hope of your answering. When are you going home?'

Very coolly Clary told her, 'The day after tomorrow. Why?'

'I want to see you. It's important. Not to you, I suppose, but to me.'

Clary heard the weariness which flattened her sister-in-law's voice into a monotone, and answered reluctantly, 'All right, then. Where will I meet you?'

'Can you come here?'

'Is that necessary?'

'I'm home because I'm not feeling well.' Quickly, perhaps thinking that Clary might refuse, Susan gave her the address, finishing, 'You shouldn't have any difficulty getting a taxi.'

'Taxis are for people with money to spare,' Clary said acidly. 'What's the nearest underground station?'

The shaft struck home. Susan began to say something, thought better of it and gave her the information, suggesting they meet by the ticket box.

'I'll be there in half an hour,' Clary told her.

Donna had been correct when she noted the resemblance in colouring between herself and Susan, but instead of Donna's bright curls Susan's hair was a deep rich auburn, so striking that it shone across the station like a beacon. Even with her perfect features sharpened by strain, Susan's beauty beckoned. In the utilitarian surroundings she was alluring and exotic, a glittering star.

'How are you, Clary?'

'Fine. Thank you.'

There followed an awkward moment which threatened to stretch into a hiatus until Susan turned away, saying brusquely, 'My flat is only a few minutes' walk from here.'

Once inside the small, pleasantly furnished flat Clary cast a quick, comprehensive glance about her before her gaze came back to Susan's face.

'Looking for Morgan? He's not here.'

'I didn't expect him to be.' Clary's voice was every

bit as defiant as her sister-in-law's.

Susan smiled mirthlessly. 'I know. If you'd thought there was any possibility of his being here you wouldn't have come near the place. Sit down and I'll make us some coffee. It will give us something to do with our hands while we talk.'

As she prepared the coffee she spoke of her work as a trainee beauty therapist, finishing calmly, 'It probably appears a frivolous career but I have always wanted to do it. I hated modelling.'

Clary nodded, listening to the sound of a siren ululating along a road somewhere.

'I'm really enjoying it,' Susan told her above the soft chatter of china. 'We do quite a lot of work with hospital patients, mental patients too. They get an immense kick out of being made up. Psychiatrists say——'

'You don't have to justify your career to me.' Clary spoke belligerently, angered by the soft, husky voice, smooth as Irish coffee.

'Don't I? Then why do you look at me as if your eyes hurt whenever you can't avoid seeing me? What do you think of me, really think of me, Clary?'

'Does it matter?'

'No, it doesn't.' She said no more until the coffee was made and poured. Then, staring into the dark depths of her cup, she said without preamble, 'I should never have married Angus. I never loved him as he deserves to be loved.'

'Then why did you marry him?' Clary knew that she sounded remorseless, but sentences from her mother's last letter danced in her brain, goading her on.

Angus is making a great effort, Helen Grey had written, *but he has lost a lot of weight. I don't think he is eating properly.* And later, *He has turned in on himself, become withdrawn. He looks so lonely.*

Susan cried angrily, 'Because he was so—so *dependable*! At the time that's what I needed, someone

I could rely on. And he loved me. I felt a responsibility to him. He didn't mean to use his love as a weapon but he made me feel guilty because I couldn't love him as much as he loved me. I know I should have been strong and refused to marry him, but he made things so easy for me. He just took charge, he was in control, I didn't even have to think! I needed that basic, rock-deep stability you Greys have.'

'It palled on you fairly quickly.'

Susan's face closed up, her expression becoming smooth and bland, her eyes as shallow as green glass. 'I tried,' she said carefully. 'At least give me credit for that. I tried and he knew I was trying and that hurt him beyond bearing. You're all so damned *intense* behind that matter-of-fact air you cultivate so religiously, even your mother. Oh, Angus tried to smother his pain and his anger, but it was only a matter of time before the anger won out over the pain. I knew it would happen and then all that intensity would be turned against me. I was frightened.'

'Don't give me that! Angus wouldn't hurt——'

'You listen to me.' Susan set her cup down with a little jarring crash, spots of colour burning high along her cheeks. 'Angus has exactly the same temper as you. Sooner or later that self-control you're all so proud of would have snapped and I'd have borne the brunt of it. I tell you, I *know*! I may be the sort of woman you despise but I happen to have a well-developed instinct for self-preservation. It slipped a bit when I let him talk me into marrying him, but it soon sprang back into life. Angus has the kind of iron integrity which smashes lesser people; he's quite capable of breaking anyone who fails to live up to his standards. I know, I lived with him, I'm not the little sister he's always loved and protected.'

Stung, Clary hurled, 'He would—he did love you, and protect you too. You forget, I saw him with you.'

'On our honeymoon. Of course he did, then. But he
didn't love me, he loved the woman he thought I was,
the woman who loved him in return.' Susan drew a
deep breath. 'Oh, what's the use? You're just as hard
as he is. You look at the world from your lofty, self-
righteous little pinnacles and wonder how in hell
people manage to make such a mess of their lives. I
only hope for your sake that you aren't obsessive like
your father was—like Angus is.'

'That's a peculiar way to excuse yourself,' Clary
said icily, her hands trembling.

Susan drank her coffee with swift, catlike neatness.
When she had finished she set the cup down and
looked steadily across the space which separated her
from Clary, her face a beautiful porcelain oval.

'Well, what if I am trying to vindicate myself?
When you saw me with Morgan you looked at me as if
I were something loathsome, something disgusting
you couldn't bear to see. Your eyes went dead and you
didn't look at me again. You looked past me and
through me as if I wasn't there, even when you spoke
to me.'

'I can't imagine why my opinion should matter to
you.'

The long-nailed fingers clung to the empty coffee-
cup, then slowly relaxed. As if she hadn't heard Susan
said slowly, 'When I met Morgan it was like moving
from black and white to colour. He didn't burden
me with his emotions. I was afraid of Angus, and
guilty. Do you know what guilt does, Clary? It
corrodes your soul, it makes you hate the person
you're betraying——'

'Oh, for heaven's sake!'

'You think I'm wallowing in self-indulgent drama-
tics, don't you? Well, you listen to me, some day you
might want to know how ordinary people think and
react. With Morgan I didn't have to worry about
breaking his heart, I knew he didn't have one! He

laughed and teased and made love like a god. Oh, your brother is good, but with Morgan there was no intensity, no responsibility. It was so easy, so exciting. I needed that excitement, that glamour and charm. I needed him. He brought me back to life.'

'Did he know you were married?' Clary's breath stopped in her lungs as she waited for the answer.

'Of course not, not at first.' With defensive brittleness Susan met the contempt which darkened Clary's eyes. 'A friend of mine persuaded me to model in a charity show. He was there. I didn't have my wedding-ring on. I went to bed with him that first night—it was like a bushfire out of control. My friend warned me that he had this thing about breaking up marriages, so I didn't tell him until after I'd left Angus. When he found out he was angry, but not for long.'

The reminiscent smile with which Susan made her final comment had Clary fighting down a surge of sick humiliation. She too had experienced the excitement that caused that glitter in the green eyes of her sister-in-law, had been dizzied by the desire which licked through her body at the impact of Morgan's potent masculinity. Images danced in her brain, images of Susan and Morgan entwined in each other's arms, of her own helpless response to him. Contempt for her weakness made her gentle with the woman opposite.

'It doesn't matter,' she said tiredly. 'I had no right to be so arrogant. It's none of my business.'

Incredibly Susan produced a harsh, derisive laugh. 'If you believe that, you'll believe anything. Did you know that he hasn't been out with another woman since he left London? For Morgan that's a record. He's waiting for you to get back.'

Clary's teeth closed on her lower lip. 'I'm not flattered,' she said, 'and I don't believe it.'

'I do. My friend in Auckland moves in the same circles, she keeps me in touch. I knew he'd found someone else as soon as he came back from Chase. He was preoccupied, and he made it quite clear that things were over. Oh, he was quite kind, very generous, and totally implacable. Before I knew what had happened I'd been paid off. I felt like the whore he obviously thought me. I insisted on going with him to that restaurant even though I knew he no longer wanted me with him, because I was furious, I wanted to meet his cousin, I thought I might find out who he was hunting.'

Clary could find nothing to say, no way of breaking into the agitated angry words. In a way it seemed that by revealing it Susan was ridding herself of the humiliation she had felt at her summary dismissal.

'Well, it served me right,' Susan went on bleakly, her normally modulated tones raw. 'He damned near ate you with his eyes, and he hated me for being your sister-in-law because it meant that you'd have nothing to do with him.'

Clary closed her eyes, recalling only too well the storm of emotion which had battered her that night. Long lashes flickered, then lifted to reveal nothing but a blue as intense and opaque as lapis lazuli. 'He behaved,' she said evenly, 'like an absolute cad.'

The words didn't sound amusing or old-fashioned. Not the way she said them.

Susan shivered at the complete lack of emotion in both face and voice. 'You sound like a judge pronouncing sentence,' she muttered.

Outside it had begun to rain again, this time the determined, weary drizzle of a London autumn. Silence, somehow eased of tension, spread through the little flat.

Abruptly, after a further quick glance at Clary's pale, shuttered face, Susan said, 'He knew I wanted to do this course and he arranged it. He was very kind, in a totally impersonal way. I suppose because he realised that he couldn't really blame me for being your brother's wife. He's very logical, is Morgan.'

'He's a swine.'

'Because he sleeps around? Then so was Angus. You don't really think that he came pure as the driven snow to our marriage, do you? Grow up, Clary. Are you still a virgin?'

Colour burned along Clary's cheekbones. Stiffly, keeping her eyes fixed on a small china dish on the table, she said, 'I don't see that my moral standards have anything to do with this.'

Susan was smiling, with surprise and a hint of sympathy. 'Poor Morgan,' she said unexpectedly, and then, 'poor Clary. At least I knew right from the first how it was going to end! Men like Morgan Caird do not fall in love, at least, not the happy-ever-after kind. They marry for practical reasons and fidelity isn't a part of the bargain. Romance is strictly for affairs. And I don't suppose he has ever made love to a virgin. He has his own principles.'

Clary said nothing. There was nothing to say. She knew, had known from her first glimpse of him, that he was nothing more than a predator, sleek and beautiful and dangerous.

'He rescued me,' Susan said abruptly. 'I wanted him and I told myself all the stupid things that women have fooled themselves with when they want to go to bed with a man they know instinctively has nothing more than sex to offer them.' Her voice changed as she leaned forward, capturing Clary's reluctant gaze in a painful kind of complicity. 'You'll find yourself doing it too, Clary. They come easily, all those lying platitudes. It must be love, you'll tell yourself, and at least there'll be memories. Don't be fooled by the traitor in your body.'

'I'm not so stupid,' Clary returned flatly. 'Anyway, I'm not likely to see him again.'

Susan's mouth curved in a sardonic smile. 'I'd say he probably knows the exact date you're arriving back in Auckland,' she said with the calmness of complete conviction.

'You're paranoid.' But Clary was uneasy.

Susan gave an odd grimace. 'I know the man, and I saw him in action. He's not a man to accept defeat, not in any part of his life. Just remember, when he holds you and tells you in that beautiful voice that he wants you, how it will end. I don't think you could handle an affair.'

'Any more than you could handle marriage.'

Susan flinched but took the thrust without anger. 'If you're a virgin you don't want to cut your teeth on Morgan. Men have the advantage over women. Angus will sublimate his anger in work and probably embark on a period of dissipation just to prove he's over me; I don't think any woman will mean as much to Morgan as his work. Don't let yourself be sweet-talked into an affair, Clary, why ask for pain?'

They had talked themselves out. For a moment they stared at each other, reaching a tenuous understanding, and then Clary got to her feet. 'I have to go.'

They walked back to the station under a grey, lowering sky.

'Autumn,' Susan said wistfully. 'At home it will almost be summer. Are you flying straight through?'

'I'm stopping off for a week in Hawaii.' Clary shrugged, suddenly bone-weary. 'It seemed a good idea at the time, but at the moment I only want to get home.'

'Oh, you'll enjoy it once you're there. Lie on the beach and polish up your tan.'

At the entrance to the station they stopped, and there was another awkward silence.

Moved by the hidden gallantry in the other woman's bearing Clary suddenly leaned over and kissed her cheek. 'Goodbye and good luck,' she said quickly.

Susan's astonishment was open and rather shaming. 'You too. If you can bear to, keep in touch.' She hesitated then said half under her breath, 'When the time is right, tell Angus I'm sorry. Not for leaving him, but for marrying him.'

Clary watched as she turned and swung off down the indifferent street, back straight and stiff, the glowing hair hidden by a scarf. As she went into the station she thought that just like that a woman might go to the gallows.

Not until she was back in her small bedroom did she allow herself to consider Susan's warnings. Brooding uncomfortably in the chair, she wondered if Morgan Caird really did want her enough to pursue her as Susan had indicated. The thought brought a half-excited, half-terrified thrill with it; she had to force the rational part of her brain back on course.

Viewed logically, of course the idea was absurd. What he wanted from her was obtainable easily enough anywhere. The dark promise of his sexuality was fascinating enough to attract all women but those in love with someone else. That sensual magnetism combined with his powerful personality made him almost irresistible.

Logic must force him to realise that there could be no sort of future for them. Unfortunately logic seemed to have very little place in the attraction which had blazed into life between them. As for any future, well, his affairs didn't deal with the future, they were very much of the here and now—and the past.

He was everything she despised in a man, a sensualist with a hunter's callous instincts and cold ruthlessness. If Susan was right and he intended to try to renew their acquaintance, he also had the hide of a rhinoceros. It would always be impossible for her to feel anything but contempt for the man who had caused Angus such heartbreak.

CHAPTER THREE

'HONOLULU was superb,' Clary said, hugging her mother. 'All frangipani and fabulous sunsets and mosquitoes! I loved it.'

'But you're glad to be home?'

'Thrilled. Like all Kiwis I'm convinced that New Zealand is the best place in the universe. You're looking extremely fit, mama. And so,' turning to her brother, 'are you, Angus.'

He smiled, nodding at her suitcase. 'Is that all you can show for the years you've been away?'

'And the backpack!'

They laughed, amusement temporarily replacing the cool wariness which each was striving to hide. Seen together they must look rather like clones of each other, Clary thought. All tall, all with the same colouring except that Angus had his father's darker skin and was superbly tanned; all three had eyes the brilliant deep blue of the sky at twilight, and the same features shaped each face, feminine grace altered to a harsh masculinity.

Quickly, to hide the fact that she was ill at ease, Clary told them, 'Actually I've sent a tea-chest back from London by sea. It's got all my winter clothes in it as well as my souvenirs.'

Suddenly swamped by love and pleasure, she smiled radiantly at them both. It would have been nice to link her arm with her mother's but Helen had never found it easy to show her affection physically, so Clary contented herself with another quick hug before saying eagerly, 'Come on, let's get out of here. I've seen enough of airports to last me ten years.'

Auckland glowed under the warm spring sunlight.

Tucked into Angus's aged, much-loved Jaguar, Clary relished the way the red roofs of suburban bungalows contrasted with trees and lawns. Coiled about the land were the estuaries and inlets of the two big harbours, land-locked Manukau and the Waitemata dotted with its many islands. Gardens burgeoned with flowers, the jewel colours of impatiens like gleaming eyes in the shade, tall wands of yellow and lollipop pink ixias, Dutch irises in the deepest, brightest blue in all the world, and graceful azaleas.

Even as Clary sighed with pleasure she sent a swift, secretive glance towards her brother. He didn't look as though his life had been shattered. He had an impassive face, hard to read; it was impossible to tell what went on in the clever, quick brain. Just now he seemed tired, the already harsh framework of his features emphasised.

'He's working too hard,' Mrs Grey confided that night after he had left for his flat. 'I'm worried about him.'

Clary looked up. Normally her mother would not dream of discussing Angus; it was a measure of her anxiety that she revealed this much.

Brusquely she told her mother of the meeting with Susan, ending, 'She seemed genuinely sorry.'

'So I should hope! Really, people like her make me so angry! Jumping headfirst into situations and then feeling sorry when things go amiss. Why on earth did she marry Angus if she was going to run away with the first attractive rich man who looked sideways at her?'

'She said she married Angus because she needed his protection. And because she felt responsible for him.'

'Because he fell in love with her?' Mrs Grey looked her disdain. 'It can't have occurred to her that he'd recover much more quickly from a firm refusal before things got too serious than he would from a blow to his self-esteem like this.'

Clary sighed. 'Was it only to his self-esteem?'

'Who knows? It has been a long time since I had any idea of what was going on in Angus's brain. It will be a long time before he forgives her.'

Helen's astringent common sense was refreshing, even if it couldn't encompass every situation. On impulse Clary said, 'I saw Morgan Caird too.'

Helen cast a swift, sharp glance at her daughter's smooth, down-bent face. It was as impassive as that of her brother. Repressing a sigh Helen asked, 'What's he like?'

'A dark angel.'

Her mother's lifted brows recalled Clary to herself. She laughed, covering the slip with flippancy. 'A big, bold pirate, modern style, sleek and elegant and super-sophisticated. Sexy as hell and well aware of it. A splendid male animal, but behind all the glamour there's a kind of cynicism which, speaking personally, scared me witless.'

'Oh dear.' Helen forbore to comment on this vivid description of a man her daughter had only seen for a few minutes. 'A dangerous man. I gather he and Susan are no longer together.'

'No, that's all over. He set her up in a flat.' Her mouth twisted in sudden savage sarcasm. 'He was very generous. It's a nice little place, and she is training to be a beautician, a beauty therapist. I gather he provided the wherewithal for that, too.'

'Well, she was always interested in that. I wonder what caused the break-up?'

Clary had never been able to lie to her mother. Now she didn't even try. Quietly she sat out the penetrating scrutiny until Helen said, 'I wish Angus had never met her.'

'Unfortunately he did, and he loved her and now he's lost her.' In spite of her efforts to control it Clary's voice was strained. She gave a sudden, wide yawn.

Helen got to her feet. 'My dear, you're exhausted. Go to sleep. Things will be better in the morning.'

Her mother saw too much, but she never pried. Helen believed in allowing everyone plenty of space, particularly her children.

The night passed in dreamless sleep. Clary woke late to a cloudless sky and a day of such calm loveliness that she spent the rest of the morning admiring it from the terrace at the back of the house.

Although Helen held a responsible position as a buyer in one of Auckland's department stores she made time to garden. After the death of her husband when she had moved her family into this house there had been nothing growing on the section but lawn and a scraggy old datura tree. The loveliness which gladdened Clary's eyes now was a tribute to her mother's care and hard work and skill.

'Oh, this is sheer, pure bliss,' Clary told the elegant bronze crane by the little fountain, eyeing with a connoisseur's pleasure the clustered blossoms of pink and white and crimson at its feet. Across the struts of the pergola a creeper suspended crimson-throated flowers like small pink trumpets.

A step below the balustrade the lawn spread out in smooth lushness presided over by a weeping cherry, bereft of blossom at this season, and several rosebushes heavy with scented blooms. Late bulbs sent flowers forth from beneath shrubs and perennials; a chaffinch flitted across the lawn and a blackbird called impudently into the warm air.

'Oh, it is *good* to be back,' Clary told a thin marmalade cat from over the side boundary. 'Now all I have to do is get a job.'

She hadn't expected it to be easy, but after a couple of weeks spent answering advertisements for quite unsuitable positions she began to wonder whether it would be better to go back to nursing. Most of the places she was offered seemed to entail vast amounts of work and responsibility for next to no wages, and several were extremely dubious.

'Hopeless,' she told Angus one night, describing one man who wanted a housekeeper and had made no bones about propositioning her there and then.

'I wish I'd been there,' Angus growled. 'What is the chance of getting a decent job? I thought the hospitals were shouting for qualified nurses.'

She shifted in her chair, watching him as he poured drinks, whisky for him, Cointreau for her. Mrs Grey was at the theatre and Angus had allowed himself to be coaxed into taking Clary out to dinner. It had been a pleasant evening, but now she felt tired and a little miserable. Angus was no longer the brother she had used to tease and be silly with. An old quotation— from the Bible?—came to mind. *The iron had entered his soul.* She could see why her mother worried about him.

'I don't know,' she said frankly. 'It looks as though I'm going to find out, though.'

He regarded her levelly, tasting his drink, then said, 'You'll get there. Look, do you mind if I put the television on? There's a current affairs programme I want to watch. One man in particular . . .'

The programme was good, incisive and hard-hitting, and Clary enjoyed it until halfway through when it switched to a panel discussion, and one of the panellists was Morgan Caird. Clary stiffened, her gaze flying to her brother's face; he was sitting like a monolith, gripping his glass with a ferocity that whitened his knuckles.

'I'll turn it off,' Clary muttered, scrambling across the room.

'Leave it. I've never met my wife's lover. I'd like to see just what he's got. Besides money.'

'But——'

'Leave it, Clary.' He spoke quietly but she shivered as she huddled back into her chair.

What followed was near torture. Morgan was completely at home in the studio, very self-possessed, the cool brilliance of his mind rather awesomely revealed. Others lost their tempers; not so Morgan. Others rambled, tried to obscure the point, justified themselves. Morgan revealed any shoddiness in their arguments with a few concise, rather curt sentences before settling back to watch them with a dispassionate, concentrated scrutiny.

Clary forgot to drink, forgot Angus, forgot everything but the need to keep her eyes on the screen, drinking in the severe beauty of Morgan's features with sheer sensual pleasure. Oblivious, her heart in her eyes, she watched until Angus got up and switched off the set.

'Well,' he said, draining his glass in one savage gulp, 'what do you think of him? She has good taste, my wife, hasn't she?'

'Angus——'

'After she left me I made it my business to find out as much as I could about bloody Morgan Caird. I wanted to see if there was any way I could pay him back.'

'Oh, Angus——'

'I'll do it some day,' he promised, coldly determined. 'I'll make him wish he'd never set eyes on my slut of a wife, never slept with her. He's six years older than me—those six years are my bank account.'

'And Susan?' When he frowned at her she probed gently, 'Are you going to make her suffer too?'

'No. She's not worth it, the cheating, lying tramp.'

Clary bit her lip, restraining herself from asking him to justify his attitude. She could tell him that Morgan was not as much to blame as he thought, but a glance at his shuttered, brooding expression revealed that it would be useless. Now was not the time to tell him what she had learned from Susan, or that she had met Morgan. Angus was too much a prisoner of his pain and humiliation to listen. The Cointreau slid smooth and fiery over her tongue; she sipped it slowly, watching from beneath her lashes as he poured another drink and stood staring grimly into it.

After long moments he lifted his head and said without expression, 'I've made a start. This latest gadget is going to take me to the big time, Clary. All I needed was a start; the consortium has given me that, and barring something unforeseen I'm going to fly far and fast. I'll end up as rich as Caird, perhaps richer. And when I've got the power I'll bring him to his knees. Hatred and the desire for revenge provide a really strong impetus to ambition.' At her horrified gasp his voice hardened even more. 'Do you blame me?'

'Revenge is about the worst reason for doing anything,' she said steadily, 'but I can understand how you feel. I hope you don't end up like him, hard and ruthless.'

'It seems to be the way to go,' he said indifferently. 'He started out with nothing much and now he's a millionaire. If he can do it, so can I. Anyway, it appears that not all women share your aversion to hard, ruthless men. He's had his share.'

Clary had never felt quite so inadequate. Damn Susan, she thought, searching her brother's closed, dark face. Angus had retreated, turned in on himself, urged on this destructive path by the sort of pain she could only imagine. As yet no one could help him; she could only pray that he would soon emerge on the other side of this dark night of his soul, with the madness of revenge left behind.

When he left she waited up for her mother, trying to make sense of the thoughts chasing themselves around her brain. Helen arrived home as she was making cocoa, trying to woo sleep.

'My dear, what on earth is worrying you?' Helen asked.

Mug in hand Clary turned to face her. 'We saw Morgan Caird on television. Mum, do you think

Angus is *unbalanced*? He spoke so—so wildly, yet he meant every word he said.'

Helen sighed. 'Put some more milk in the pan, there's a dear, I'll have some with you. No, I don't think he's unbalanced, just coping with a very complex, painful set of emotions the only way he knows how to. He feels very deeply, so his sense of betrayal is—well, I suppose extreme is as good a word as any. He needs time to come to terms with himself.'

Clary certainly hoped that time was all he needed. When he arrived at the house the next afternoon she scanned his face unobtrusively but carefully. He looked a little aloof, perhaps, as if he were embarrassed by his outburst of the night before, but otherwise just as he always had. Only—his eyes were like stones, opaque and flat.

'One of the men I deal with in the consortium knows a woman who's recovering from a heart attack,' he told her after his greeting. 'Apparently she lives with a son who has to travel a lot so she needs someone to take responsibility for her. More like a companion than a nurse, I gather. It's live-in.'

'It sounds all right,' Clary agreed cautiously.

'If you want it you'll have to go and see her.' Long fingers searched through pockets, finally emerging with an address. 'There's her name, and the hospital ward. She's expecting you at two tomorrow afternoon. Why don't you want to go back nursing, Clary?'

She hesitated, frowning unseeingly at the slip of paper. 'It's hard to explain, but at the moment I want something less structured.'

'Do you want to find yourself?' His tone invested the words with a mockery which had grown sharp and punishing.

'No,' Clary said softly, thinking of Susan and her unhappy face. 'I know who I am and what I am. I'm good at my profession and I'll probably go back to it fairly soon. But I need time to assimilate all that I did

while I was away. I need to wind down.' She grinned
and gave his lean cheek a teasing little pat. 'You
should know what I mean. In your spare time you
devour travel books—*Forty Years Spent Crossing The
Sargasso Sea*, et cetera, et cetera.'

His sardonic expression eased into laughter.
Hooking a powerful arm around her waist he swung
her from one side of his body to the other. '*Touché*.
I'm glad you're home, love. It's been a lonely few
years.'

And although her heart ached for him she knew that
he had said all he ever intended to say about his brief
marriage.

Mrs Hargreaves was not a big woman but she
managed to dominate the hospital lounge without any
effort at all. She watched Clary approach with shrewd,
snapping eyes, surprisingly youthful in her elderly
face, and a small smile.

'My son told me you'd be in,' she said by way of
greeting after Clary had introduced herself. 'What sort
of music do you like?'

Clary's swift, radiant smile was touched with
mischief. 'Classical, with the exception of most violin
concertos and some string quartets, opera, especially
Italian, some pop, some country and Western,
Victorian music hall songs——'

'Very eclectic.' Mrs Hargreaves' smile widened.
'And have you a sense of humour?'

'Banana-skin variety? Certainly.'

'How about a joke against yourself?'

Clary smiled rather ironically. 'Well, I can usually
see the joke,' she admitted. 'Sometimes I laugh. Once
or twice I've even thought them funny.'

'Miss Honesty. When can you start?'

Startled, Clary suggested, 'Don't you want to check
my credentials or look at my references, or something?'

'My dear, if you are inefficient or dishonest, or I

discover a secret passion for heavy metal rock in you, I'll get rid of you soon enough, don't worry. What do you know about the job?'

Clary told her. Mrs Hargreaves nodded, her eyes never leaving Clary's face. 'That's it exactly. You'll be paid a nurse's wages, you will be on call for most of the time until I can manage to convince my son that I have no intention of dying this time, and I plan to be fully recovered in three months' time.'

'I've no doubt you will be,' Clary assured her. 'I knew that the job was temporary.'

'Well, can you start tomorrow? I don't want to spend a day more in this place than I have to.'

Still bemused, Clary gave a sudden chuckle. 'Very well, but I'll leave my references and papers here and you must promise to read them before you and your son make a final decision. Am I the only person you have interviewed?'

'No.' Mrs Hargreaves' tone consigned all the other applicants to perdition. 'I don't need your bits of paper, I've made up my own mind all my life and rarely had cause to regret it, but if it makes you happier to leave them here, do so. I won't read them. Clary is an odd name. Short for Clarissa?'

'I was named Clarice after my grandmother,' Clary told her with a grimace, 'but fortunately my brother decided on Clary and it's stuck.'

'It's unusual, like you. Pretty. I like it. I'll see you at the address on that paper tomorrow at three. Goodbye.'

Torn between amusement and astonishment at being so summarily hired Clary left, stopping on the way home to buy some summer clothes. The ones she owned were a little tired and a size too big; six months ago she had been some pounds heavier. Because the Crowes had insisted on paying her a substantial bonus she had a comfortable sum of money in the bank, but habit persuaded her to shop carefully. She did not mind paying for quality, it was just that the years spent overseas had curbed any tendency to extravagance.

A pair of sandals completed her purchases. They were a little difficult to find but after several false starts she discovered a pair which fitted her, although she pulled a face at the price. Still, the position of the straps lent elegance to her feet; women with feet out of the norm had to pay for comfort, and hers were narrower and longer than average.

Promptly at two-thirty the next day she climbed down from the bus, smiled thanks to the driver when he handed her a small suitcase, and walked briskly to where, as promised in Mrs Hargreaves's phone call of the night before, a car waited. At Clary's appproach a middle-aged woman got out, her smile wide, warm and uncomplicated.

'Clary Grey?' When Clary nodded that smile deepened and she held out a competent hand. 'I'm Ruth Swann, Mrs Hargreaves's housekeeper. Hop in. Did you have a good trip up? Just as well I decided to come out a bit early. The bus can be pretty erratic but it's not usually ten minutes ahead of time.'

'There were no trucks holding us up on the hills,' Clary said, deciding that she was going to like Ruth Swann.

'It can take much more than half an hour to get this far, although with that new stretch of motorway to Albany things are much better now. I'm afraid this next bit of road is the worst part of the trip. Still, it's not far.'

She drove slowly inland down a narrow gravel road, carefully avoiding the thick build-up of metal on the side. Clearly she did not feel confident enough about the road to indulge in idle chit-chat. After a few minutes Clary decided that she trusted her driving enough to take notice of the unfolding landscape. About them low hills were spotted with sheep and red

Hereford cattle sheltering from the sun in the shade of trees, some still chewing at the lush grass. A little stream ran between banks decorated with the tall wrinkled trunks and spiky heads of cabbage trees. Clary inhaled as the heavy scent of the great panicles of tiny cream blossoms floated in through the window.

After a mile or so the road debouched into a valley, fertile and well-farmed, with hedges and clumps of trees providing shelter and beauty.

'Almost there,' Ruth Swann said. 'Look, you can see the homestead from here.'

Clary followed the direction of her nod and felt her heart swell. Pink and severe against the spreading green of the enormous trees behind it, the house stood well back from the road at the end of a long drive. She had seen enough Georgian houses in Britain to recognise the style immediately.

'It must be very old,' she said, her eyes fixed on it with a shock of something that was almost recognition.

'It is. When Mrs Hargreaves and her husband—that was her first husband—bought it, it was almost derelict. Over the years she's completely restored it. The garden, too. People come from all over the world to look at the garden. She's a real fusspot about details, and everything in the house and the garden has to be just so. I really don't know what she's going to do now that it's complete.'

Clary was quite sure that Mrs Hargreaves knew exactly what she was going to do. She was far too decisive not to have made plans to cover any such eventuality. She said nothing, however, watching with satisfied eyes as the car moved beneath the magnificent magnolias which lined the drive, the rusty under-surface of the leaves barely moving in the slight wind. Beneath them were rhododendrons and azaleas, past their best now but still colourful, sheltered from the worst of New Zealand's winds by a belt of native evergreens along the fenceline.

Clearly her new employer did not lack money. A housekeeper did not come cheaply, and the gardens which unfolded before her appreciative eyes were far too extensive to be kept in such immaculate condition by one woman, however vigorous.

Clary leaned back into the solid comfort of the Volvo. That there were extremely rich people in New Zealand was no secret; normally they kept a very low profile. It seemed that in the next three months she was destined to find out how one such family lived.

Her eyes roamed lovingly over the restrained façade of the house, its severe simplicity and the perfection of its proportions enhanced by the faded pink of the weatherboards.

'It took Mrs Hargreaves ages to find just the right shade,' Mrs Swann confided as she guided the car around to a complex of buildings behind the house. 'At first the painter thought she was crazy, but she soon changed his mind! In the end he was as fussy about it as she was.'

'It is perfect.'

Clearly the buildings which housed the Volvo and, judging by their area, other vehicles, had once been the stables. They were separated from the house by a wide stretch of ground which held an orchard and a flourishing kitchen garden. To one side, screens and lush plantings sheltered a swimming-pool. A large space paved with flags led into the house.

Clary took a deep breath of the warm air, spicy with the scents of stocks and thyme blossom, and said simply, 'I think I'm going to love it here.'

'I hope so,' the housekeeper said crisply. 'It can be a bit isolated if you are used to city living.'

The winged line of Clary's brows lifted but all she said was a pleasant, 'May I see Mrs Hargreaves now?'

'Well, the doctor gave her a sedative and when I left she was asleep. I'll show you to your room and on the way I'll have a peek to see if she's woken yet.'

'It doesn't seem to me that Mrs Hargreaves needs either nurse or companion,' Clary said ruefully as she followed the older woman up a superb flight of carved stairs and down a wide hall lit by the sun through a pair of French windows.

'Oh well, there's enough for me to do here just keeping the dust under control! And the doctor thought she needed someone here to make sure she didn't get back to work too soon. She's not used to sitting around. Until she had this trouble with her heart she lived for her garden. I think they thought she would get bored and restless.'

Clary gave a non-committal nod but she remembered the sharp intelligent eyes of her employer and decided that Mrs Hargreaves was surrounded by people who fussed too much. She did not seem the sort to decline into apathy. Far from it, she possessed altogether too much shrewd common sense to allow herself to become bored.

'Here's your room. It's right next to hers and there's a bell—see, here—that she can use to call you if she needs you. Now, after I've seen whether she's awake I'll make us a cup of tea while you unpack. Or would you rather have coffee?'

'Tea will be fine, thank you.'

'I'll bring it up on a tray. You must be ready for it.'

This switched Clary's stunned gaze from her perusal of the lovely room. 'Oh no, you won't,' she said decisively. 'I'm not here to make extra work for you. After I've unpacked and had a quick shower I'll find my way to the kitchen.'

'Well, if you're sure.' Mrs Swann was doubtful. 'The bathroom—it's your own little one, you don't share—is through there. We've a bore as well as good supplies of rainwater, but it is only spring and there's all the summer to get through yet, so if you could be economical with the water . . .'

'Of course.'

Mrs Swann left the room, only to tap on the door a moment later to assure Clary that her employer was sleeping like a baby. When she had gone Clary smiled and set to unpacking, putting her clothes into the drawers of a superb wardrobe—surely not *genuine* Sheraton?—which was so much more fitting than a modern built-in would have been.

Either Mrs Hargreaves or her decorator had chosen green and a fresh primrose yellow for the room, warmed by the amber of an immense Persian rug which almost hid the wide polished boards. The furniture bore the deep patina of age and care, the little davenport in the window reflecting Clary's bemused expression as she stood for a moment looking through the panes.

'Beautiful,' she told the room, her gaze lingering on the wide four-poster bed with its embroidered spread before she went into the tiny, luxurious bathroom and showered off the dust of her journey.

Half an hour later she ran her fingers through the bronze waves of her newly dried hair, smoothed the skirt of her shirt-waister and went out of the door and down the hall, following her intuition towards the kitchen.

The house was silent, all doors open to the mellow spring day. In the downstairs hall sunlight spilled across the crimson rug and the dark floorboards, and winked from a silver vase holding an arrangement of pink blossom. Clary tensed, setting her feet down carefully, as quietly as she could because there was a watchful, waiting quality to the atmosphere.

The soft thud of a door closing behind her brought her to a frightened halt. Every fine hair on her body prickled upright; her hands tightened into fists while her heart pounded as though she had just seen the monster at the core of all nightmares.

'Come here, Clary.'

She struck one clenched fist into the wall, willing

the pain to free her from the sick anger which held her captive.

'Clary.' This time there was concern in the hard pirate's voice.

'Damn you, Morgan Caird,' she whispered through bloodless lips, turning at last to face him, 'how dare you use my brother to get me here? How *could* you!'

'I would have used anyone, including my mother,' he said, his dark gaze purposeful as he reached for the hand she had maltreated. 'But in this case you can blame coincidence for your arrival here. Or the Fates.'

It was useless to resist. She watched dully as he ran his thumb over the knuckles, smoothing the tender skin with something like relief. She kept her eyes lowered but she had seen that he too had lost weight in the past months. He looked tense, wound up to too tight a pitch, the heavy-lidded eyes burning as they swept her shuttered face with possessive fire.

'Come into the office,' he commanded quietly, leading through the open door.

Once there he gestured at a chair but when she resisted the mute suggestion he opened the door of a cabinet which held bottles and glasses. He poured brandy and brought it to where she stood in the centre of the room, her whole being clamped into stiff rejection.

'Drink this,' he ordered, holding the glass to her lips.

Numbly she drank, not even choking as the warming, life-giving cognac slipped down her throat. When it was gone she stayed silent, the dark blue of her eyes opaque, every freckle standing out across the bridge of her nose as she stared over his shoulder.

'Now you can shout at me,' he said urbanely.

When she ran the tip of her tongue across her lips that flicker of relief lightened his expression once more, but Clary was too beleaguered in her own private hell to be aware of it.

'I'm going home,' she said huskily after long, silent moments.

'No.'

The monosyllable fell with heavy emphasis. She looked up into that possessive glitter she dreaded and feared.

As if awakening from death she said, 'You can't stop me.'

'I can.' He set the glass down and took her hands in his, holding them to the thin cotton of his shirt, just above his heart. The heavy beat drove into her palms, fast and irregular, a counterpoint to the turbulence of her own.

'Clary,' he said so thickly that her attention was dragged from her long fingers up to the drawn, intent passion which spread over the symmetry of his features until the sign of the predator blazed forth, fiercely intent on his own needs, his own desires.

'No!' she cried, but it was far too late. He crushed the little sound beneath his lips, smothered it into nothingness with the primitive intention of forcing a surrender.

Knocked completely off balance by his reappearance Clary lost control, drowning in a purely pagan response. Her mouth opened, every bit as savagely desirous as his; she clenched her fists into the crisp material of his shirt, uncaring that her grip might hurt.

At last the ferocious kiss ended; red lights dazzled beneath her closed lids as he muttered, 'Oh Christ, I need this,' against her mouth before demanding on a muffled half-laugh, 'Do you know how long it's been? Centuries, an aeon of waiting . . .'

Clary couldn't answer. Absorbed by the signs of arousal in the lean body pressed so intimately to hers she turned her head and began touching small kisses to the damp, slightly salty skin across his cheek until she reached the slashing line of his jaw.

Her mouth was erotically open, the tip of her tongue leaving a small trail to mark the position of each kiss. His scent of man was more beautiful to her than anything a flower could produce; it filled her nostrils. Heat bloomed to life deep within her then rioted in tendrils of sensation through her body. For the first time she realised that desire can produce as complete a self-absorption as pain. At that moment she lived solely through her senses. All thought processes ceased; she understood only the ache in every cell, the throbbing urge to submit and so to master. A groan shuddered the length of her throat as she twisted against his aroused body.

'Stop it,' he said heavily, 'unless you want me to take you here, on the floor.'

His voice was empty of emotion, as though he was producing sounds to go with someone else's thoughts, but the words struck through the sensual haze enveloping Clary. She froze, the ache in her flesh becoming an anguish of frustration before she jerked free of his hold, her set face white with self-hatred at the betrayal by her body of heart and mind.

'Oh—God!' She pressed her fists to her eyes but nothing could shut out the hardening of his expression or the triumph there.

'I don't know why, either,' he remarked conversationally, regaining command of himself much more rapidly and easily than she did. 'However, one of the many things my tough and sensible mother taught me was never to waste time bewailing facts. Like it or not, *we* are a fact. If we had met in the ordinary course of events you would have followed your inclination and not that particularly obstructive conscience of yours, and we'd have gone on from there. Now that you're here you'll be able to learn that I am not the villain you think me.'

Slowly she lowered her hands, staring at him with the flat, unwinking gaze of hatred. 'Why should I want to know you? I know what you are. That's quite enough for me.'

He met her eyes with an implacable determination which reduced her defiance to fear. 'You know nothing about me.'

'I know enough to prevent me from sleeping with men who seduce my sister-in-law,' she whispered.

For a moment she thought she had found a chink in his armour of self-possession. A muscle at one corner of his mouth was pulled tight, straightening the sensuous curve, but before he spoke it had relaxed.

'I don't suppose you have met many,' he said calmly. 'She is not promiscuous. Or are your morals so firmly rooted in the nineteenth century that you consider any woman who has an affair to be a harlot? If so, you're a hypocrite. That's no virginal reaction I get from you.'

She hated his cynical appraisal, hated the reminder of her flaming response to him, hated, *hated* him. Stonily, her expression bleak, she stated, 'I'm going home.'

'You are not.'

The even, toneless statement sent a nervous chill through her but she lifted her chin to demand, 'And how do you propose to stop me?'

'Quite easily.' He took a step towards her, stopping with a frown at her involuntary tremor. His hand dropped and he said, 'I'd rather not use force to keep you here but if I have to, I will. Make no mistake about that.'

'How?' she asked, hiding an icy trickle of fear with contempt. 'You can hardly keep me in chains——'

'How much do you love your brother?'

The silky interruption silenced her as nothing else could have. Every muscle in her body clenched in anticipation of a blow. 'Why do you ask that?' she whispered.

This was how he must conduct business, with a

pitiless assurance which delivered either a *coup de grâce* or an infusion of capital in the same cool manner.

'What has Angus to do with—oh!' Realisation hit her in the blow she had been expecting.

'Yes,' he said judicially. 'When Angus wanted financial backing for his latest idea he approached a friend of mine. He was interested, but unable to help him, so without giving him my name he contacted me, knowing that I'm always interested in possible exports. I investigated Angus very carefully and was impressed. While this was under way I met Susan. Her name meant nothing to me, there are plenty of Greys about.' His lips twisted derisively. 'I wish I had never set eyes on her, but she seemed to be free, she was certainly available and even you must admit she is very beautiful.'

'Is that all that mattered to you?' Clary's voice was shaking with outrage. 'That she was beautiful?'

'No. I liked her, she was amusing and intelligent. I was angry when I discovered that there was a husband, but by then she had left him. She never spoke of him, so it came as a shock to discover that he was my genius inventor.'

He hesitated and Clary said as nastily as she could, 'The opportunity to make money being more important than any woman, however good in bed she is?'

'Strangely enough, no.' He spoke mildly, patiently, as though she was being very obtuse but she rejoiced in the gleam of anger beneath his lashes. 'Your brother's invention has the capability to save lives, Clary. And, if it is developed here, to earn the country a considerable amount of money. As soon as I made the decision to back him I set up the consortium, covering my tracks so that he doesn't know that I *am* it. Solely, entirely. I can withdraw my support any time I like. Angus was too eager to get the backing to worry about terms. It will be almost impossible for him to go anywhere else for development funds.'

'Why?'

He told her, reducing the technicalities to a clear statement that Angus had more or less handed over the marketing rights to the consortium. 'Which means that there are few financial sources open to him. Anyone who provides funds for development will only do so for the rights to market it.'

'Did you do this deliberately?' she asked, white-lipped.

He hesitated. For a moment she scanned his implacable face with painful intensity.

'It's standard procedure,' he said at last, dark lashes hiding any emotions he felt. 'He's a genius, your brother. As for today ... I knew when you were coming home, but it never occurred to me that you wouldn't go back to hospital nursing. My financial frontman mentioned my mother to him after Angus had told him how difficult you were finding it to get a job.'

'But you knew before I came here today.'

'I knew before you went to see her.' Again he hesitated, the fractional pause so at odds with his normal self-assurance that she stole another look at him.

In profile he was just as beautiful as full face; she wondered with an aching heart why she had never considered any other man to be beautiful. Yet allied to the symmetry of features and the subtle harmony of colour, gold of skin, green of eyes, delineation in black of brows and lashes, warm tawny tint of hair, there was strength and character. It was the character which was in evidence now, a certain grimness which straightened the finely moulded mouth into harshness.

He looked up, catching her helpless scrutiny, and his eyes darkened, one hand going out towards her. For a moment their glances locked; then he shook his head to clear it and said abruptly, 'I didn't expect contacting you to be this easy, but it's happened, and I'm not letting you go.'

'How can you stop me?'

'I can still pull the money out.' He nodded at her startled gasp. 'I told you that he was eager to get the backing. If I do that, as well as having no wife, he will find it extremely difficult to perfect the one thing that is keeping him sane at the moment.'

'How do you know that?' she cried in a hard hoarse voice, turning away from the inexorable strength and purpose of the man.

'I know,' he said. He smiled, but there was no amusement in the bright depths of his eyes.

'All this because of a woman?'

'All this because of you.' He corrected her bitter question with the patience of a hunter who is confident of his chance to kill. 'So what are you going to do? Tear back to Auckland in high and righteous dudgeon, or stay here?'

Outside the sun beamed down on newly-mown lawn, calling forth that indescribable, delicious perfume of freshly-cut grass. A thrush not long out of the nest hopped importantly about underneath the long leaves of a bush. Clary's eyes followed the brilliant flash of colour which was a parakeet as it sped towards the orchard so fast that the red and blue and green of plumage was a blurred streak. Its loud 'quink-quink-quink' fell in familiar cadence on her ear.

'I won't expect you to give yourself to me as a sacrifice for your brother,' he remarked, investing the statement with an insolent mockery which tore at her nerves, 'I won't insist on anything. When you come to me I want it to be a willing surrender. All I ask is that you give us time to get to know each other.'

He came across to where she stood motionless, putting a hand on her shoulder to turn her towards

him. 'For example, until my mother told me
yesterday, I'd have said that Victorian music hall
songs and you——' The smooth voice was cut off as
his finger lifted her blind face. 'Clary,' he muttered,
holding her close to the warm length of him, 'don't,
darling, please don't. I don't want you to be
unhappy——'

'Will you let me go?'

'If I do, will you go out with me?'

Her eyes flew open to meet the grave question in
his. 'No,' she whispered.

He gave himself no time for thought. 'Then my
answer is the same. No. You stay here.'

'You have yourself a bargain.' That dreadful
unseeing anguish was gone. With a dignity which
made her suddenly formidable she disengaged herself
from his grasp and he, perhaps recognising that she
had reached the limits of her control, let her go,
although his brows shadowed his eyes in a frown.

'Very well,' he said crisply after a tense moment. 'I
don't want either your brother or my mother to know
about this.'

She bit her lip. About Angus she could only agree;
her heart quailed within her at the thought of his
reaction if he should find out any part of the truth.
Slowly, as if considering the matter, she said, 'I could
try a little counter-blackmail.'

'Threaten to reveal my perfidy to my mother?' He
was smiling, genuinely amused. 'My darling, my
mother entertains no illusions about me. Anyway, she
would think it a perfectly rational way to behave. I
told you she was tough, and very practical. Much
tougher than you, because you couldn't do it. You're
far too conscious of your duty to your patient.'

Her shoulders slumped as she made a small defeated
gesture. 'Too soft, I think you mean,' she said
tonelessly. 'Luckily for you. May I go? I did promise
Mrs Swann that I'd have tea with her.'

CHAPTER FOUR

THEY met again in the small drawing-room before dinner, Clary still pale but hiding her maelstrom of emotions with an air of cool poise which she hoped only she knew was barely skin-deep.

She was standing in the long window watching a kingfisher on the top of a melia tree, admiring the brilliant blue and buff of its plumage against the cloudy lilac flowers. She had dressed carefully for this confrontation in a rose-pink skirt and matching shirt, looping a silver chain about her neck. It was not her custom to wear much jewellery, and when she did it was always silver. Gold tended to look obvious against the sheer translucence of her skin.

When the door opened her nerves tightened, warning her of Morgan's entry. She refused to look around.

'How did you find my mother?' He spoke quietly, pleasantly, but there was an inflexible quality to his tone which forced a careful answer. Clary realised that he loved his mother very much.

'She appears to have suffered no ill-effects.'

'How did you manage to persuade her to stay in bed?'

Clary shrugged. 'You implied that she's a realist. I merely pointed out that if she over-exerted herself now she'd almost certainly pay for it tomorrow.'

'What are you staring at so desperately?' He spoke from just behind her, his silent passage across the room startling her. 'Ah, our local *kotare* in his favourite hunting spot.'

'I thought they ate fish.'

'As an occasional treat. I've seen kingfishers with

mice and lizards in their beaks, but mostly they prey on insects and worms. He'll have a hole full of hungry nestlings in some bank quite close by. Ah, there he goes.'

A flash of the bright blue to which he gave his name, then the little hunter rose from the lawn with encumbered beak and sped back through the trees.

'And now,' Morgan said very softly, 'would you like a drink before dinner?'

Up in her room as she dressed Clary had made a very firm decision about this man. She had decided that she would treat him with the courtesy due an employer and her host, and she would, in all her dealings with him, assume an aloofness which would keep him effectively at bay. She would be polite and reserved and answer him when he spoke to her; she would not volunteer information or conversation, and she would make sure that he never got the chance to touch her.

Her strange and probably irrational conviction that she could trust him, at least when he said he did not want to force her to do anything other than stay here, had helped her make that decision, although not without a surge of fury because he had made that concession in the arrogant belief that he had the power to persuade her easily into his bed.

The long months since they had met had not diminished her body's perverse hunger for him, but she had forgotten its strength. Now, with him only inches away, his subtle male fragrance taunting her senses, she realised sickly that the ease with which she made decisions in her room was belied by the violence of her reaction to his presence. It was going to take all her will to control the leaping response in her blood.

His suggestion of a drink brought relief. It would get him away from her long enough to stop the fine trembling in her limbs.

'Yes, sherry please,' she said, her voice abrupt with strain.

'Dry, of course.'

Mockery, of course.

'I like all sherry,' she told him politely as she followed him part of the way across the lovely room. Beside a glass-topped curio table was positioned a lone chair. Pretending to be fascinated by the mementoes so carefully arranged beneath the glass, Clary sank on to the cushion.

'A truly civilised appreciation of the wine.' Morgan's voice was urbanely sardonic as he set a glass on a table beside a luxurious sofa.

For a moment they were perfectly still until his hard handsome face broke into an ironic smile at the swift mutiny in Clary's expression.

'I don't want to have to shout across the room,' he said softly and held out a hand to her.

Eyes clear as the sky on a summer midnight measured the crystalline glitter of his, clashed and held in fierce silent battle. When Clary rose it was a defeat made more bitter because she had been fighting her own instincts. Behind his worldly mask lurked a throwback to more barbaric times. He would not have forced a physical surrender; he did not need to, because they both knew that once in his arms she lost all sense of personality and became a slave to their mutual passion.

Still smiling, he came across and lifted her to her feet; she had to suffer the small punishment of his hand at her elbow until she sat in the place of his choosing. Lesson one, she thought drearily. Do as the man says.

The wine was pale and dry. At first it made her shudder, but in a very short time she learned to appreciate the austere flavour. With her face in three-quarter profile she gave polite non-committal replies to his polite non-committal statements.

He hadn't sat down beside her. His point made and taken, he chose a chair opposite, and watched her. The impact of that survey stretched every nerve on a rack, but she set her teeth and endured it stoically as he commented on the headlines, told her a little of his mother, and a little more of this place which was to be her prison.

'Very prosaically known as Hunter's Valley,' he said. 'The first settler was one James Hunter, who arrived a hundred or so years ago with a pregnant wife and all the paraphernalia necessary to live the life to which he'd been accustomed, that of an English gentleman. Unfortunately common sense wasn't part of his equipment, nor adaptability, nor, I regret to say, any inclination for hard work. He took one horrified look at the valley, half swamp and half bush, and fled to Auckland where he lost his money in unwise speculation.'

'Careless man.' Clary concentrated on relaxing her muscles before their tension became painful. 'Did he sell the valley?'

'No, no one wanted it. Eventually his son, a much more far-seeing and practical young man, decided to do something about rebuilding the family fortunes. When he was eighteen he left his parents to their genteel poverty in Auckland and came up here. He built a *nikau* hut where the homestead is now and set to work bringing in the land.'

Unwillingly she had become interested in these pioneers. 'Was it he who built the house?'

'Yes. It was as close a replica as he could get to the ancestral home. You must have seen quite a few of the originals in your perambulations about Britain.'

'Yes.' Seen them and loved them, loved the way the timeless felicity of their severe proportions, solid yet graceful, acted as the perfect complement to the gentle loveliness of the countryside they adorned.

She said as much and he nodded, watching her from beneath his lids. 'We like to think it suits our landscape as well. A very adaptable style.'

'Mrs Swann said that your mother had restored the house and the gardens as well.'

'It's her hobby. Unfortunately there's very little for her to do here now.' He cast a glance around the serene, gracious room. 'When my parents bought the station both the land and the house were in very poor heart. It took them years and an immense amount of money and hard work to get it back into shape. My father died before it was done.'

Why was he telling her this? Intuition gave her the answer. He was trying to establish links between them, encouraging the exchange of information. It was difficult to hide her resentment at this attempted manipulation, but she was well-schooled in manners and appropriate responses seemed to come without thought.

'How old were you then?'

'Eleven.' He smiled, the hard mouth rueful. 'Old enough to be a damned nuisance by considering myself the man of the house. My mother packed me off to boarding school.'

'That seems a little harsh.' She spoke tentatively, for a moment forgetting all her reasons for mistrusting this man in her compassion for the child who had lost his father so young.

'I told you she was realistic,' he returned coolly. 'I thoroughly enjoyed school, as she knew I would, and left determined to try some other way of earning my living than farming. The financial world fascinated me. By then my mother had married Geoffrey Hargreaves, so it was just as well I'd decided my future lay in Auckland.'

'Didn't you get on with him?'

'Not particularly.' He sent her a smile of cynical tolerance. 'I was quite prepared to like him, but he felt that his extra years and his position as my stepfather gave him certain rights. Rights I wasn't prepared to concede. I was young and rash, he set in his ways and conventional.'

'That's—rather sad.'

'Oh, we didn't quarrel. Nothing so undignified. We just didn't see much of each other.'

'When did you come back here?'

He looked at her. 'When he died.'

The answer told her a lot, even delivered as it was without inflection. He had resented those years in exile, but the hard practicality which was one of his legacies from his formidable mother had helped him accept that they were necessary.

'I went to university,' he said, watching the changing emotions in her face with hooded eyes. 'Then with an enormous amount of cheek and a stake inherited from poor old Geoffrey, I took on the financial establishment. I enjoyed it immensely, the wheeling and dealing, pitting my wits against all comers, the incredible deals—it was like riding in an exhilarating circus, but by the time I reached thirty I decided to turn respectable.'

She couldn't prevent the laughter which bubbled forth at his wide, shark's grin. However hard he tried to 'turn respectable' there would always be something of the pirate in him. Something she had better not forget, she thought, appalled at how easy it was for him to make her laugh. As she snatched the smile from her face she reminded herself that this man had seduced her sister-in-law, and was not above using blackmail to get his own way.

'You look much prettier when you smile,' he observed, not bothering to hide the lazily caressing note in his voice or the slow appraisal which accompanied it. 'When you're angry your eyes light up but you go white around the mouth and your face gets a pinched look. I want to see you smile a lot while you're here.'

'Oh, I can grimace like a trained chimpanzee,' she retorted. 'But that's all you'll ever get.'

That shark's smile altered in quality, all of his

ruthlessness and the cold intelligence which fuelled it displayed in the handsome face. 'You'll do what I want,' he told her calmly. 'Dance, smile, talk——'

'Make love?'

'Not unless it's what you want,' he answered, the green-gold eyes completely confident as they rested like a kiss on the controlled line of her mouth. 'You've set up barriers in your mind, but I can wait until they're down. I don't go in for rape.'

'What is this you are doing to me if it's not some sort of rape? You force me to stay here, to acknowledge you——'

'That's what frightens you, isn't it?' He moved into the attack with the smooth deadliness of the predator he was. 'You don't want to see me as a man, no more nor less than any other man. To you I'm an ogre, the beast who stole your brother's wife and is forcing you to stay in my lair. But you're running scared because when I touch you you become mine. In fact, I don't even have to touch you. Look at me.'

As if they were dragged upwards her lashes lifted. She stared into his narrowed eyes, her skin prickling with instant heat as he deliberately let his gaze drop from the length of her throat to the curves beneath the rose-pink shirt, and thence to the long legs tucked gracefully against the sofa. By the time the sensual assessment was over her mouth was dry and her body feverish, her expression twisted by shame.

'All I have to do is look at you,' he said, no mercy softening the deep voice, 'and you become mine. Every response of your body belongs to me. And that is what scares the hell out of you.'

Her tongue touched the centre of her top lip. His gaze lingered on the small betrayal and tension roared across the space separating them like the lightning she had once seen blow a tree apart. It had all the casual inevitability of a primal force.

'It's the same for you,' she managed to return

raggedly. She was barely able to form the words but something had to be done before she was dragged to her feet by this almost irresistible desire and went to him in silent surrender.

'Yes,' he replied, his voice uneven, 'but I'm not fighting it, Clary. I know what I want and I'm going to get it. You'll find that desire eats at your guts until it becomes an obsession. Do you know I haven't had a woman since I saw you? I haven't even wanted one. Have you slept with anyone since then?'

The question hit her like a fist smashing glass. Mesmerised, she shook her head, seeing too late the triumph which blazed over the hard features. At that moment she crashed to a full realisation of the power and potency of his masculinity. Her eyes dilated as he came towards her; she could not move, her whole being trapped by such naked hunger that she was not surprised to hear his breathing, the feral sound of a man forced by passion back to his primitive self.

This time he did not just extend a hand. His fingers fastened on to her shoulders and he pulled her to her feet, his chest rising and falling as though he had climbed a cliff to reach her. His eyes were slits, his face drawn and famished but he held her away from him until she signified defeat by closing her eyes and swaying close to the lean strength she craved.

She expected the crushing brutality of their last embrace, was prepared for it, would have welcomed it. Indeed, his arms closed about her like a vice but instead of taking the soft mouth held for him he buried his face in the hollow where her neck joined her shoulder as if her warmth and closeness was enough.

Clary's hands moved slowly, pulling his shirt free from his trousers. They ached to touch his skin yet she could not hurry them; they seemed enclosed in some medium thicker than air which impeded movement and sensitised her skin.

When at last she slid her fingers beneath the

material of his shirt his mouth moved convulsively against the heated silk of her throat. Trembling, she stroked the sleek warmth of his back, her shudder answered by his; a small, bland smile as old as the first woman pulled at her lips and forced the lashes down to cover her blank, unfocused eyes. Beneath the slow exploration of her hands his skin was on fire, smooth and silken over the taut framework of his body, magnificent, perfect to her.

A little gasping noise rattled in her throat. She turned so that her mouth came in contact with his neck and she pressed an open kiss there. Untutored, guided purely by instinct, her hips began to move, seeking relief from the burning ache which consumed her.

'Oh *God*!' he muttered, responding ferociously to the provocative, unconscious movement. His arms tightened as his hands slid down to her hips and brought her hard against him.

Clary went up in flames, welcoming the fierce thrust of his loins with an ardour as potent as it was explicit. She had no experience, no comparison to make. In the past there had been occasions when she had fought her way free from embraces as ardent as this, but they had caused her nothing but an uncomprehending disgust. She had forgotten them.

There would be no forgetting this, no convenient banishment of the sensations running untamed and free through her body, the straining, desperate urgency which had her reciprocate in kind. Her arms clung tightly across his well-muscled back, her mouth nuzzled into the part of his face or neck which was nearest as she tried to press closer, seeking that unknown, ultimate ecstasy with every movement.

'If I kiss you I'll take you.' The words were thick, rough, and they made no sense.

Clary didn't know that she was whimpering, strange, wild little noises expressing nothing but her pleas to have this pain assuaged, this hunger sated. The man holding her released her, then just in time to prevent her falling he grabbed her shoulders, shaking her with a violence which snapped her head backwards.

'Clary,' he groaned, more clearly this time, and again.

Slowly her lashes lifted, revealing empty, brilliant eyes. Colour burned along her cheekbones and her lips were parted, the tip of her tongue just visible.

Morgan's dark face was under such savage stress that it looked like a mask carved from dead wood. Strong white teeth clenched in agony; as awareness returned to her his chest rose and fell abruptly, the breath breaking harshly through his lips. He was not looking at her, he stood staring above her head. Clary tried to move away but her steps faltered. Already painful fingers gripped her more tightly, bruising her flesh.

In a voice she did not recognise she asked, 'Has this ever happened to you before?'

'No. Never.'

As the urgency of passion began to seep away, cooling her blood and taking with it the terrifying demands of a need she did not understand, she began to shake with reaction and self-contempt.

'Why?' she whispered. 'Why you, of all men?'

He smiled bitterly at the white hatred in her face. 'Why not? One of Fate's little jokes, my lovely. Can you stand upright without support yet?'

She needed to hide from his knowing gaze but her feet only took her as far as the nearest chair. Huddled into it, she watched as Morgan drained the rest of his drink and brought hers across. It was no consolation to see that his fingers trembled slightly, or that dusky colour still burned beneath his skin.

Her body was racked with unfulfilled longing. Hastily she drank the wine and sat hunched over the empty glass. 'I don't believe it,' she said blankly. 'It doesn't happen that way. I don't believe it.'

'Refusing to believe it in the hope that it might go away doesn't work. I spent some months trying.'

She barely heard him, her mind trying to make sense of the whole situation. Slowly, as if they might get hurt in the process, her eyes drifted towards Morgan. He sat down, the muscles in his thighs flexing and then relaxing as he stretched his legs in front of him. Another wave of heat scorched through Clary as she remembered those strongly-muscled thighs against hers and the exquisite sensations they had engendered.

'It's impossible,' she protested jerkily. 'It's *indecent.*'

He met her accusing stare with a great burst of laughter. His head went back in open enjoyment while Clary watched in impotent and fuming silence.

'I wonder what your definition of decent is,' he teased when his amusement had faded.

She shook her head, more affected than she dared admit by his laughter. 'You know what I mean.'

'Yes, I do. Doesn't it make you wonder, the fact that we can almost read each other's thoughts? No, I can see that you're going to try to close your mind to that too, just as you've refused to accept anything else about this situation.'

'All that you want me to admit is that I want to go to bed with you!'

'I know that you do, I've always known it. And so have you, from about two seconds after we saw each other across that pony ring. No, I want much more than your reluctant admission of desire, Clary.'

'You want me to be your lover,' she said angrily.

His soft laughter held a caressing note which tightened the skin over her cheekbones, across her breasts. 'That's inevitable,' he said with cool arrogance, 'but that won't be enough. I want all of you. All the intelligence and spirit and character, all of the warmth and the kindness—everything. All of it, just for me.'

Horrified, she stared at him. The freckles across her nose were like tiny exclamation marks on her pale skin.

'You're crazy,' she managed at last.

'Ambitious, perhaps; not crazy. You see, not only do I want you—I've had to face the fact that I must have you.' He gave a twisted, enigmatic smile, the classically perfect features rendered suddenly as harsh as a hawk's profile. 'Which was a considerable shock——'

'You might well end up wishing that you'd never seen me,' she interrupted. 'What if I demand the same of you?'

Arrested by the fierce challenge flung at him like a glove in the face, Morgan's expression revealed his surprise. Then it was replaced by that imperturbable mask which so successfully hid his emotions.

He replied, 'I think I would be disappointed if you accepted less. You're welcome to take what you want of me.'

'Be careful it's not your soul.'

Later, eating strawberries in the dining-room, she watched his lean hand lying motionless, half-curled on the dark polished wood of the table and wondered with shame just what had possessed her to succumb to a dramatic urge.

An excess of emotion—of sensation. Even now she felt the nagging bite of unsatisfied passion. How easy it would be to rouse again the tiger which slept so lightly within her.

A swift upward glance revealed Morgan's face, remote with the implacable beauty of great sculpture. Deep inside Clary, hidden tension dissolved in a surge of unidentifiable emotion.

It terrified her. *He* terrified her. She knew exactly

how the defenders of some great fortress must have felt when the walls they trusted to save them proved useless against the assault of treachery. Naked and bereft, betrayed by an enemy within.

The glowing crimson strawberries were tasteless in her mouth. Nervously she swallowed, forcing her mind away from the frightening present to the immediate past, to Mrs Hargreaves.

'Don't look at me as though I'm a patient,' she had greeted Clary when she had gone in to see her and found her awake. 'Tomorrow I'm getting up.'

'No reason why you shouldn't, if you remember that over-exertion now will set you back tomorrow.'

The shrewd eyes, more hazel than her son's but with the same straight brows, were fixed on Clary's face. 'Oh, I shan't overdo things. I don't intend to die for quite a few years yet. I'm going to see my grandchildren before I go.'

'An excellent ambition, and one quite easily attained if you do as you're told until you are over this,' Clary had replied, but her shock must have shown in her face because Mrs Hargreaves chuckled.

'It's time Morgan settled down. He's had a good innings, now he's ready to indulge his dynastic urge. You met in London, I believe?'

She couldn't have made her satisfaction more obvious if she had come right out with her blessings.

'Just outside,' Clary said hastily. 'At Chase.'

'Nice place, isn't it? Pity my cousin is such a stupid man. Still, his wife is even more stupid.' Mrs Hargreaves dismissed the Sedburys with open contempt. 'Do them both good to have to work for a living. Do you think you're going to like it here?'

Clary thought bitterly of that obsessive desire which carried within it the seeds of its own destruction and said carefully, 'Yes, I'm certain I shall. It's a lovely place.'

'But the people don't appeal so much.'

It was on the tip of Clary's tongue to tell her just what she thought of one of the people there, but she remembered Morgan's threat, and her own sense of responsibility forbade her to disturb the woman in the bed. So she said merely, 'I'm afraid it takes me a little while to relax with people I've just met, but everyone has been very helpful. Very nice,' she finished lamely.

'Of course they have,' Mrs Hargreaves said with relish. 'Both Morgan and I like living with nice people, probably because we're not very nice ourselves. Do you believe in the attraction of opposites?'

Clary avoided the shrewd gaze of the older woman by straightening the flowers on the bedside table. 'I'm afraid I've never given it much thought.'

'Try it some time. Thinking, I mean. It's amazing how few people are actually capable of thinking, as opposed to using their emotions as reasons for their actions. Morgan has a very good brain, he's always used logic as a basis for his actions. So far it's worked extremely well for him, but although he probably doesn't realise it, he's vulnerable because he doesn't know how to cope with the sort of emotion which goes beyond logic. Now, off you go and get dressed for dinner. I don't want to see you again tonight. Ruth Swann is going to get me up to date on the Valley gossip.'

'I'll come in before I go to bed.'

At this juncture there was a slight tussle of wills, which Clary won. Now, drinking excellent coffee, she wondered at that remark about grandchildren. She had assumed, in the most egotistical way, that it was aimed at her, but perhaps Mrs Hargreaves had some other woman picked out to be Morgan's wife. Savaged by a jealousy so intense that it hurt to draw breath, she had to set the coffee-cup down. It made a soft chinking noise as it reached the saucer.

'What is it?'

His voice startled her into looking across at him.

Something in her expression gave her away, for he got to his feet and came to crouch by her chair, taking her hand in his.

'What is it?' he repeated half beneath his breath, his thumb finding a pulse which fluttered wildly. 'Do you feel ill?'

'No, it's nothing.' She tried to free her hand but his grip tightened. Seen so close his eyes were actually a green as deep as the sea; from the dark pupil the green was irradiated by rays of gold like a sunburst.

Beautiful eyes, superbly shaped and placed in the sculptured framework of his face, heavy-lidded, with long curling lashes. Very slowly she reached out a finger and traced a straight black brow, the haughty aquiline blade of his nose, the sweep of cheekbone, until her exploration reached the autocratic jaw. Still staring into his eyes as if lost in their depths she followed the line from his ear to the thrusting strength of his chin. She was overcome by a strange tenderness which mingled with the effect of his closeness to become inseparable from it.

'You are magnificent,' she heard her own voice whisper as if she had discovered the answer to the riddle of the universe.

He didn't smile. Like her he seemed astonished, almost awed at the newness of this experience, but the glitter of gold in his eyes flared to a radiance she could not meet.

'And you are perfect,' he said at last, his voice husky.

It was then that the barking of several dogs roused them from their absorption in each other. Beneath her fingers Morgan's lips moved as he said something she was glad she didn't quite catch, then he was on his feet, listening as the noise of a car engine increased, idled, then stopped.

It was a man to see him on business of some sort; they spent an hour in the office, emerging as Clary was wrestling with the intricacies of a country telephone exchange.

'Wait,' Morgan said curtly to her. 'I'll be back in a moment. Use the phone in the office.'

'I'm quite capable——'

But he was sweeping the rather surprised visitor away with him, only to reappear almost immediately.

'Look, you needn't bother——' she began angrily as he opened the door into the office.

'It's no bother,' he returned, his mocking amusement only too obvious. 'As your host it's my duty to smooth your path whenever possible.'

'You're not my host, you're my employer.'

He smiled. 'Is this the number you want?'

'Yes. It's my mother. I'll reverse the charges.'

He lifted his brows. 'My dear girl, we can afford a call to Auckland.'

Clary frowned, and he leaned forward and said, 'I've spent a lot of time these last months wondering how you'd look when you smiled. You don't do it enough, but the reality more than lives up to the best my imagination could produce. Actually, I've been living a rich fantasy life since I met you. I've derived an immense amount of pleasure imagining you in all sorts of ways——'

'Stop it!'

'——laughing, smiling that funny little smile you give when you try to hide the fact that something has amused you, naked and eager in my bed, in my arms——'

'Morgan, shut up!'

His voice overrode her shocked protest. He stood by the big desk, one lean hand on the telephone, and effortlessly held her rooted to the floor by the sheer power of his words. 'And afterwards, when you're sated, I know how you're going to look then, too. All that self-control you wear like armour will have disappeared, and you'll be open to me. Your skin will be flushed and your lashes will curl down over your eyes and that lovely mouth will be fuller, still red from my kisses. And your beautiful body will be warm and lax, and mine, all mine . . .'

Fascinated, terrified at the punishing surge of desire roused by the slow, erotic words, Clary's tongue touched her lips. The brilliant gaze which held her prisoner caught fire at the involuntary little movement. He took a step towards her, his intention plain, and then stopped.

'No,' he said raggedly, 'this is not the time, or, damn it, the place. When we make love we're going to have all night to do it and a bed to make it comfortable. Otherwise you'll end up so bruised that you won't be able to move for days.'

'You are incredibly conceited if you think it's going to be that easy.' She didn't really know what she was saying. She was too busy trying to conjure up some self-control so that she could subjugate the unruly sensations which went brawling through every nerve and cell in her body.

'Face facts.' His voice was dry and sardonic; by now he had his emotions well under restraint. 'I can take you any time I want to. I don't even need to touch you to have you completely willing. But you must be ready too, because once we become lovers it will be too late to change your mind.'

'Just make sure that I don't make you wait too long.' Yes, that had the right note of contempt to it.

He looked very levelly at her, meeting her accusing stare with a touch of her own contempt. 'I can be patient when I want something as much as I want you.'

'I'm not a *thing*!'

The broad shoulders lifted slightly. Clary watched as he strode behind the desk.

'I'm sorry.' He sounded tired. 'No, you are not a thing. You are all woman. My woman. But I like my fruits mature, not sour and unripe. So I'll wait.'

CHAPTER FIVE

HE did not leave the room while she spoke to her mother. He lounged on the other side of the desk with a moody expression which intrigued while it irritated her. Halfway through the call it was replaced by a smile, taunting and amused. She had to suppress her savage desire to slap it from his face. Only worry at his possible reaction and the shaming knowledge that she was quite incapable of resisting him, whatever he did, kept her hand by her side.

The extremes of emotion and sensation he induced in her were mind-boggling. Never before had she felt anything like this anger which fountained through the top of her head, and she had not known that it was possible to suffer such erotic tension. The only thing that eased her bewilderment was the knowledge that Morgan too was dealing with something outside his experience. And that was a dangerous path for her thoughts to take. She could not afford to weaken. His need for her surrender was all that kept her safe. If he came to her room at night she would accept him as her lover and while they were together she would give him everything he desired.

But afterwards she would hate him and hate herself, and he knew it. Because he was the man he was, possessive, dominant, he needed more than the begrudged gift of her body. *All of you*, he had said, and he meant it. He wanted capitulation, to take over her life like a conqueror. So he would not press her to sleep with him, not yet.

Submission was impossible. If she allowed him any sort of victory she would lose herself. Exactly as her father had, as Angus had. She was terrified of becoming an emotional cripple like them.

When the call was over she slammed down the receiver, glaring at him.

'Very cool,' he said, those penetrating eyes sliding over her angry face. 'Are you always so matter of fact when you speak to your mother?'

'We aren't a demonstrative family,' she snarled, then bit her lip.

'No?' The single syllable said it all, but in case she had missed the point he hammered it in. 'I know one of you who is—very demonstrative. Excitingly so.'

'That's sex,' she scoffed. 'Not emotion. I've seen what emotion can do.'

'Angus?'

'And others.'

He came around the desk and slid his fingers around her wrist. 'So you are afraid.'

'Aren't you?'

'Yes. I knew that sort of emotion existed; my parents were devoted to each other. I never thought it would happen to me.'

Stunned, she pulled her wrist free, twisting to stare up into his face. 'Are you implying that you are in *love* with me?'

'How do I know? I've never experienced it before. You'd be pleased if I loved you, wouldn't you, because it would give you power over me.' Her eyes blazed, and he smiled without humour. 'You'd pull the world down around our ears and glory in it, if you thought it would free you from me.'

In the days that followed she expected him to press his claim but although he insisted on her company whenever he was home he didn't touch her except with those bold, disturbing eyes.

In an odd way she enjoyed herself. Mrs Hargreaves was well on the way to complete recovery and her astringent common sense made her an entertaining if occasionally intimidating companion. After one sharp enquiring glance she made no comment on the tension she picked up when Clary and Morgan were together. When she wanted her face could be as impassive as Morgan's.

After the first uncomfortable few days Clary found herself taking pleasure in the times when all three were together. Accustomed as she was to her mother's calm practicality, the unsentimental frankness between Morgan and his mother pleased rather than shocked her. Nor did she make the mistake of underestimating their affection for each other. She listened without horror as Mrs Hargreaves told Morgan exactly which sort of tree she wanted her ashes buried under.

'A Charles Raffil magnolia,' she told him firmly, ignoring his smile. 'The one with those superb rose-pink flowers. Plant it down by the water-lily pond. The empress tree will be too big by then, it will have to come down before its roots block the drain. I can't think what possessed me to plant it there. Not that it matters, as I've planted another by the tennis court.'

'I wish you would make up your mind,' Morgan complained cheerfully. 'That's the fourth one you've chosen in the last year. Every time a new catalogue comes out you fall in love with a different tree!'

'Ah, but I always go back to my lovely magnolia. It is, I think, one of the most beautiful trees in the world. Just think, every year you'll be able to go out and tell each other how well I'm flowering!'

Repressing her surprise at being coupled with Morgan so blatantly, Clary said, 'Or that it's a blooming good year for mothers.'

This brought forth some satisfactory groans as well as a crop of puns from the other two, each worse than the one before, until she clapped her hands over her ears and cried peace.

Mrs Hargreaves busied herself with one of her catalogues, making a list as she scanned the pages. It was Saturday and Morgan lay sprawled on a lounger, reading the newspaper. They had just finished morning tea beside the pool. The sun beamed down with the fresh, hopeful strength of early summer. Both women sat in the vine-wreathed shade of the pergola but neither the heat nor the dancing, glinting light from the pool seemed to bother Morgan. He didn't even wear dark glasses.

Clary had been watching him for some time before she was aware that she was taking in the shadows cast by those long lashes, the loose-limbed grace of his relaxed body, the way the muscles in his leg moved when he pulled up one knee to balance the sheets of newspaper. The beautiful morning had coaxed him into wearing shorts and a loose cotton shirt, but he looked as elegant in them as he did in his severe, well-tailored business suits.

Desire tightened into a coil in the pit of her stomach. Before she could look away his lashes lifted and his eyes met hers; in them she saw a reciprocal passion. The peace of the morning fled.

'Come for a swim,' he said, too calmly.

'I only swim at the height of summer, when the water is lukewarm.'

'The solar panels on the roof keep it that temperature all year round.' He recognised the excuse for what it was and gave her no quarter.

'I haven't a bathing suit.'

His smile slid over the edge into mockery. 'We always keep spares. Ruth is easily shocked, so we prefer that no one swims naked.'

He got to his feet and came across to where she sat, feet pressed side by side, knees and thighs primly clamped together, her whole body tight with rejection. 'We're sure to find one that fits you,' he insisted and pulled her gently from her chair. 'I'd like to see if skin as white as yours ever tans.'

His touch burned into her arms. She said, 'Mrs Hargreaves . . .?'

Without lifting her head the older woman said, 'Go and swim, Clary, or he'll pester you until you do. Morgan always gets his own way. It's very bad for his character, but that's the way he's always been.'

'So come on.' The silky voice laughed at her impotence, but there was an intense hunger in his gaze which seemed to fill an emptiness in her.

'Very well,' she said under her breath.

Like children they walked hand in hand past the huge room which was used, so Ruth had told Clary, for informal parties. It was furnished in cane and light wooden furniture, rough yet elegant and comfortable, and had its own kitchen facilities and the same quarry-tiled floor which formed the terrace around the pool.

The changing-room was just as luxurious. Clary surveyed the shower cubicles, the wide bench which served as a vanity, and the enormous mirror. There were plants here as well as in the party room, great leafy things which emphasised the impact of dark wood and more quarry tiles. It could have been a grotto beside a pool in some lush, tropical jungle.

'Here,' Morgan said, opening one of a bank of cupboards. 'See what you can find. If you aren't ready in five minutes I'll come in to get you.'

She opened her mouth to protest but he was already halfway to the door. Frowning to hide the piercing excitement in her blood, she eyed the bathing suits carefully stored in the cupboard. Her frown deepened as she pulled out various scanty pieces of swimwear, holding them up before discarding them. Bikinis would expose far too much skin to Morgan's bold appraisal, yet the only maillot which was long enough in the body and big enough in the bust for her was one with exceptionally high-cut legs which she disliked.

A quick glance at her watch made the decision for her. Even as she hissed with dismay she tore off her clothes and climbed into the clear yellow suit. It didn't need her swift look at her reflection to reveal that the suit hugged her body far too lovingly. Ordinarily it would not have worried her to wear such a maillot; what tensed every muscle was the fact that Morgan had definite effects on her body and she was at enough of a disadvantage without letting him see just what he did to her.

So she headed straight for the pool and dived smoothly in before setting off for the other end in her efficient crawl. Morgan was already in the water and, like her, he seemed content to do lengths until they had both worked off some of the pent-up sexual energy which pressured them.

At last Clary hauled herself up on to the bottom step and pushed her hair back from her face. As if she had given a signal Morgan followed her, the sheen of the water accentuating the powerful grace of his body. He wasn't panting but Clary could see the rapid beat of his pulse in his throat and knew that her own was a similar betrayal.

'That suit,' he said gravely, 'could make old men's homes redundant.' He grinned at her astonishment and continued, 'They'd all die of heart attacks, or rocketing blood pressure or just sheer chagrin because you're the same age as their granddaughters. I'm rather thinking of having a heart attack myself. Fortunately I don't have to worry about the chagrin, because you're just the right age for me.'

'How old are you?' It was inane, but it was all she could think of to say while his narrowed devouring eyes were telling her that she was beautiful, that he wanted her beyond all reckoning.

He smiled. 'I'm thirty-three. And you are twenty-five. As I said, just the right age. Are you cold?'

'Yes,' she lied. His satisfied laughter followed as she showered and dressed. His confidence bordered on egoism, she told herself savagely, but the fact that he had every reason for that confidence made her cringe.

Angus, she thought stubbornly, and into her brain

there flashed an image of Morgan and Susan, the tanned litheness of his body blending into the sinuous grace of hers in the closeness of passion.

It seared savagely through her but she kept it in her mind, forcing herself to remember that even if she was so weak as to give herself to him, it would be impossible. The pain he had caused Angus with his casual lust for Susan stood between them like a poisoned sword.

'Angus,' she said through the soft hissing of the shower, repeating his name like a charm, like a warning.

When she re-emerged into the sunlight Morgan was lying on his stomach on the lounger, apparently asleep, still clad in his brief black bathing suit. Her eyes swept the length of his body from the sleekly-muscled shoulders to his lean flanks and the strength of his thighs. He lay deceptively relaxed like a great cat, with an underlying alertness which was probably never dormant. In spite of the caution she had given herself her mouth dried. For a moment her face was illuminated by such naked need that it seemed to flame forth.

She felt ill, especially when her eyes slid to meet his mother's. It did not help that there was sympathy in the hazel gaze so openly watching her. She felt cheap as well as sick. Did Mrs Hargreaves think that Morgan and she were having an affair? It humiliated her to be classed with the women who had shared his bed. She wanted to shout, 'I am special, he said so,' and immediately wondered if he told them all that.

And as immediately she recognised that her cynical little thought was unfair. Morgan was just as astounded by the depth of attraction between them as she was. He had not lied; she would have known if he had.

After lunch, when she was alone with her employer, she said hesitantly, 'Mrs Hargreaves, I am not Morgan's mistress.'

'I know that.' Mrs Hargreaves's acerbic voice softened as she went on, 'If I have learned anything in a life spent dealing with cantankerous, bull-headed, unreasonable humanity it's never to interfere and never to take sides.'

Clary said carefully, her eyes very dark in her white face, 'I didn't want you to think that there was anything going on behind your back.'

'You're a well-brought up girl. Thank you. However, Morgan is not intimidated by me. If he'd wanted to install a mistress here he'd have done it quite openly.'

'And you wouldn't object?'

Mrs Hargreaves's thin shoulders lifted. 'Why should I? Hunter's Valley is Morgan's, he can invite anyone he likes here.'

'Oh, I thought—I'm sorry, I assumed it was yours.'

'No, his father left it to him.' The older woman smiled reminiscently as she looked back down the years. 'His father was another one like Morgan. He bought the station when it was so run down nobody would come near it. The previous owner made his living by chopping the *manuka* scrub and selling it for firewood. Once we'd paid for the place we had no money for development, so we had to do it the hard way.'

'How old were you when you came here?' So interested was Clary that she didn't even consider the rudeness of her question.

'Seventeen, straight from school.' Mrs Hargreaves laughed at Clary's stunned face. 'I knew what I wanted; my parents tried to coax me into waiting by offering me a trip around the world, but I said I'd wait until John and I could go together.'

'And did you go?'

'No. He died. My splendid, vital John, gone in three weeks with a cancer he never knew he had. I'm glad I refused to wait until I was twenty-one before I married him.' Remembered pain showed briefly in Mrs Hargreaves's expression, was as swiftly banished by a definitely mischievous twinkle. 'Not that I really had much choice. John was eight years older than I, and like Morgan, he didn't wait around once he'd made up his mind. He was hard, he made a bad enemy, but he was the best husband in the world for me. And a good father to Morgan, although they had some almighty clashes. Even when Morgan was a child they were too much alike to live comfortably together. I used to wonder how I was going to cope when Morgan was growing up.'

She looked across at Clary with a grim little smile. 'But John wasn't there to see his son grow up. He would have been proud of him. Instead there was Geoffrey Hargreaves, who was shocked by Morgan's hard-headed attitudes even though he liked and respected him. Geoffrey was always more than aware that in Morgan's eyes he didn't measure up.'

Clary would have dearly liked to ask why Mrs Hargreaves had married again when she had so obviously buried her heart with Morgan's father, but she didn't dare.

'Because I liked him,' the older woman answered the unspoken question with a subtle little smile. 'And because I was lonely; because he had loved me since he first met me fifteen years before. For several reasons, but mainly because the thought of never loving again terrified me. We had a good marriage, even if Geoffrey failed lamentably to tame my wild son.'

There was nothing to say to that. Clary pushed a curl back behind her ear and twitched the coverlet straight.

'You're going to have to develop a little toughness yourself if you want to deal with him,' Mrs Hargreaves astounded her by saying. 'You have the same streak of wildness, well camouflaged of course——'

'Wildness? Oh, come on now ...' Clary laughed, her hand indicating her shirt and skirt, restrained, almost prim.

'I said it was well camouflaged. You had better accept it,' her employer said drily, 'otherwise you're going to be badly disadvantaged in this game you're playing with my son. One of Morgan's strengths is his ability to home in on weaknesses. It doesn't matter whether he's dealing with a company or a conglomerate or a man. Or a woman. He's not above using those weak points to get the results he wants, either.'

'No.' Clary was almost tempted to confide in her. She went so far as to look her way with a hint of entreaty, but even before she met Mrs Hargreaves's bland gaze she knew that she would not beg for help. She doubted very much whether it would be granted; if it was she would refuse it. She was, she had to be, strong enough to fight for herself and win. The exhilaration of battle flamed in her expression, transforming it.

'Yes, you have plenty of courage,' Mrs Hargreaves decided in a satisfied voice. 'Learn your strengths and don't underestimate your weaknesses. That's the only advice you'll get from me. Now, away you go. I'm going to rest. You can go out, if you're feeling housebound. Take the little car if you want to explore; Ruth tells me you're an excellent driver. And she will keep an eye on me, so you can have a few hours off without it hurting your conscience.'

Clary no longer worried about her patient. She was progressing well and not given to foolishness. In fact, with Ruth in the house no nurse was needed. Clary had suggested to the doctor the previous day that she was superfluous, only to be told rather austerely that as Ruth was not confident enough to take the responsibility and Morgan spent most of his time in Auckland, her presence was very necessary.

Morgan's time in Auckland was news to Clary.

Since her arrival he had slept every night at Hunter's Valley, even those on which he stayed in town for dinner and didn't arrive home until late. His deep if unspoken love for his mother was the most endearing thing Clary knew about him. It made him a little more approachable.

He did not look in the least approachable when he emerged from the office as she was going past; he looked tired and angry. However when he saw her he smiled, his eyes roaming her face with open appreciation.

'That's a very determined expression. I like the way your chin lifts in a delicate little defiance when you see me. In fact, I like all of that chin. Especially that cleft. Very provocative, I find that cleft.'

'Oh, to to hell!'

He laughed, his teeth very white in his tanned face. 'I suppose it's always a possibility. Come for a drive with me.'

'No, thank you.'

'But I insist.'

She measured glances with him, her chin very much in evidence until he smiled and said, 'I promise I won't touch you. Not unless you ask me to.'

He doesn't have to *touch* you, her brain told her and she read his knowledge of that unspoken admission in his face. He knew that even the thought of him was enough to set the blood running wildly through her body.

Yet she said, 'Where—what will I wear?'

'You look stunning as you are. I've been neglecting my friends lately, but yesterday I was pinned down by one for tonight. You'll like the Oxtens. They live at Orewa.'

'Your mother——'

'Thinks it a marvellous idea. It's been over a week since you had a day off. We'll be there for dinner but it will be a barbecue, so if you want to change, something casual.'

Casual chic, no doubt, not the sort of thing Clary owned much of. However she did have a shirt-waister in dark blue cotton which was not too elegant for a barbecue. With a wide grey belt to make the most of her slim waist and interesting pewter buttons, it could go almost anywhere.

In her room she changed and was pulling a comb through the tumbled mass of her hair when her door opened and Morgan strolled in as though he had every right.

'You damned well knock!' she flung over her shoulder.

'I did, but you were too busy muttering to yourself to hear me. What's the matter?'

'Oh, it's just my hair. It's so thick it drives me crazy.'

He came across to stand just behind it. 'I like it,' he said, looping a finger through one soft curl. 'It's like silk. I love the way it swings when you walk, and I find it intensely erotic against my cheek when I kiss your throat. But,' quite matter of factly as he released her, 'I find everything about you extremely erotic, as I'm sure you must be aware.'

'You've made it more than clear.' She had to get away. It took an effort of will to put the comb down and walk across the room to slip on a pair of dark blue sandals.

'Not going to reciprocate?'

She recognised the lazily insolent note in his voice and shook her head, caution warring with anger. 'Don't torment me, Morgan.'

'Why not? You and your inhibitions torment me.'

The words frightened her, yet she couldn't subdue the primitive pleasure which welled up in her.

'Yes, you like that, don't you?' His eyes narrowed as he surveyed her face. 'Beneath that cool restraint you're a tease, my lovely. I don't mind, in fact, I enjoy watching you spin your plots, but remember one thing. You are not going to renege on this hand. I'll collect when we're both ready for it, and the payment is going to be wild and sweet and loving for both of us.'

'Loving?' The word splintered between the syllables but she retained enough control to flash scornfully, 'You don't know the meaning of the word.'

He said quietly, 'Making love is what it's called.'

'*Sex* is what it's called.'

Beneath the fine cotton of his shirt his shoulders moved in a dismissive shrug. 'Have it your own way. Call it sex or making love, it's those and more, but it comes to one thing in the end. You are going to admit that you need me as much as I need you.'

'You'll be waiting a long time.'

He looked suddenly demanding and possessive. 'I can stand it if you can.'

The statement made her bristle, but behind the arrogant words she heard the same aching hunger which made her nights restless, the days long and tense. Her lips trembled; she turned her head so that all he could see was a remote profile.

'In the meantime,' he said coolly, 'I tantalise myself by imagining things.'

Her head snapped around before she could stop it. He was laughing at her, mockery gleaming beneath his lashes. 'So far we've made love in every different way there is, and several which are probably only described in Kama Sutra——'

'I will not be used as material for your sordid fantasies!'

The amusement was wiped from his face as if she had slapped it. 'I don't like the word sordid. Making love may be sordid to you—to me it is an affirmation of love and life, something valuable and beautiful.'

She bit her lip but came back gamely, 'I suppose you were in love with every woman you've slept with!'

'No,' he told her, 'but I have liked and respected

each one, and making love has always been a part of that. Now, Miss Prim, on your way. I love that pretty blush but we'd better get out of here before I start translating an occasional fantasy into reality.'

CHAPTER SIX

THE Oxtens lived on the cliff to the north of the long pale sweep of Orewa beach, overlooking both Orewa and the equally lovely though much smaller Hatfield's beach. Before them lay a wide, shimmering expanse of the Hauraki gulf, flecked by the multitudinous sails of a part of Auckland's fleet of pleasure yachts.

The house was modern, starkly crafted so that it seemed to hover between the enormous voids of the sea and the sky. It was impressive and very lovely, but Clary found the Hunter valley homestead's elegant suavity more satisfying. However, the Oxtens were more than happy with their house, and were certainly delighted to see Morgan.

He introduced Clary as his mother's nurse and companion, which effectively changed the knowing look in Sam Oxten's eyes into a slightly startled glance, one which he shared with his wife. Clearly they were accustomed to meeting Morgan's girlfriends, but were not too sure how to treat a woman who was not in that category. The little hiatus lasted only a second until Fay Oxten remembered her duty as a hostess.

'How is Mrs Hargreaves?' she asked as she led them into a huge room which appeared to have as two of its walls only the sea and the sky.

'Fine,' Morgan said briefly, adding with a dry lack of expression, 'you know my mother. You could, perhaps, do her some damage with a hammer if you really tried.'

'Incredible, isn't she?' Fay's voice revealed genuine awe. 'Now, Clary, meet Karen Graham and Tony— you two know Morgan, of course, but this is Clary Grey.'

The Grahams were both statuesque blondes, the woman only an inch or so shorter than her brother. From her Clary received a pleasant smile and greeting, but Karen Graham's attention was fixed on Morgan and there was that in her glorious eyes which made Clary furious. Not another one, she thought savagely as she smiled and exchanged greetings with Tony Graham.

Appalled by the violence of her angrily possessive reaction, she didn't notice the warm admiration in Tony Graham's expression until she was sitting beside him on a very expensive and rather uncomfortable sofa.

'. . . long at Hunter's Valley?' he was asking.

'I've been there since Mrs Hargreaves came home from hospital, and I'll go when the doctor decides she doesn't need me any more.'

His smile flirted openly with her. 'Where are you from?'

'Auckland.'

'So am I.' He made it sound as if it was an incredible coincidence.'

'As it's the biggest—the *only*—city around, I don't find that altogether surprising.'

'Don't be like that,' he implored. 'I was trying to forge a bond between us.'

'Consider it forged. We both come from Auckland. We're both human beings. We both speak English. Lots of bonds if you look for them.'

Using his body to shut out the rest of the room he complained, 'You're not taking this at all seriously! If you're going to be frivolous and flippant how can I possibly convince you by the time you leave tonight that you know me well enough to go out with me?'

'You can't,' she said promptly, smiling because though he was a fast worker he was rather endearing. All open and on the surface, with nothing of Morgan's dark danger. 'Now, behave yourself. It's bad manners to turn your back on the rest of the room.'

'Not when the rest of the room has Morgan Caird in it,' he grumbled, but he moved back obediently, saying with a long-suffering note in his voice, 'I suppose you're just like all the other women I meet, including my very persistent sister. You're crazily in love with the man.'

Morgan's voice was amused as he brought a long glass of some white concoction over to her. 'Alas, I wish she was,' he said lightly. 'The lady is very much her own person.'

'Oh, well, if your celebrated charm hasn't worked, go away and let me try,' Tony commanded with cheerful rudenes.

'I'm still here,' Clary said very gently, the merest edge of steel sharpening the words.

It was enough to startle Tony. 'Was I being rude? Sorry——'

'You were both being rude.'

Morgan's eyes gleamed with sardonic appreciation as Tony said earnestly, 'You're beginning to remind me of the lady who taught me when I first went to school. She had flaming eyeballs and stood fifty feel tall, and she had a nasty knack of stripping your skin at a hundred and fifty paces. Was she a relation?'

'Almost certainly,' Morgan drawled, holding out an imperative hand to Clary. 'Leave this amiable clown to his drink and gladden Sam and Fay's combined hearts by admiring their view.'

It was an order, and one she obeyed as she realised that the others in the room were paying a considerable amount of attention to them. He released her hand immediately, but not before his fingers closed around hers in a sudden fierce warning. Colour touched her cheeks; she knew she should not have let Tony corner her like that, so she walked meekly across the ceramic-tiled floor to the enormous walls of glass.

Her gasp of delight was all that her hosts expected. 'Oh, this is superb,' she breathed as her eyes took in the scene below.

The house was built back from the edge of the cliff and there was no garden, just a grove of *pohutukawa* trees, flashing green and silver in the slight breeze. Beyond them were the waters of the bay backed by Hatfield's beach and directly opposite sprawled another headland like their own, pine- and *pohutukawa*-clad, with tiny beaches at the base of rusty, cave-spotted cliffs. On the other side stretched the long gentle curve of Orewa, on this hot day thick with sun-worshippers. Past it Whangaparoa peninsula probed into the waters of the gulf. Most if it was as heavily built-over as the flat land behind Orewa beach, but the maritime park at the tip and the island beyond that were still green, as were the hills behind Hatfield's beach.

'It must be like living in the gondola of a balloon,' Clary murmured at last.

Fay nodded enthusiastically. 'Or on the bow of a ship. At night it's superb. We love living here.'

'It reminds me a little of Greece,' Clary said. 'The stark hills and the pines—only here they're much thicker and the hills are greener than I ever saw in Greece, but the olives have that silvery gleam, like the *pohutukawas*, and the atmosphere is almost unbearably the same. I drove a funny little van up a goat-track in the south of Paros and got out and cried amongst the thyme and oregano and cistus because I was so homesick.'

'Did you?' Karen was openly incredulous. 'I never got to Paros, but I adored Mykonos. I never wanted to leave it.'

Everyone chimed in with their favourite holiday spot, everyone but Morgan, and Clary, who felt rather embarrassed at her revelations. She tried to concentrate on what was being said, but her attention was almost totally captured by the man who stood beside her, outlined against the sun by an aura of light. She looked blindly at whoever happened to be speaking but she comprehended only the full oppressive weight of his watchfulness. Slowly, as inevitably as it always was, her body responded with an expectant, vivid awareness.

'How about you, Morgan?' Karen favoured him with her lovely smile. 'You've probably travelled more than the rest of us put together. What is your favourite place? Some secluded hideaway in the Seychelles? A ski-lodge in St Moritz?'

'A little village not far from London,' he drawled.

'Don't be infuriating. Tell us why.' Karen's smile was a nice blend of encouragement and languor. She was a very pleasant woman, but at that moment Clary could have pushed her out of the window without an atom of regret.

'I have a remote cousin who lives there,' he said with a tantalising smile. 'It's very pretty in the English style, but my favourite spot is one field where they hold pony-club events.'

When it became clear that he wasn't going to continue Fay Oxten pleaded laughingly, 'Oh, go on, Morgan, you great tease. We're all dying to know why.'

Speak for yourself, Clary thought, rigid with tension. What was he going to tell them? She kept her eyes fixed unseeingly on the splendid view, waiting.

He grinned at his hostess, saying with infuriating blandness, 'I first saw the love of my life there, of course.'

The laughter which greeted this was guarded, as though they weren't sure whether he was joking or not.

'Truly?' Karen said sweetly, recovering from her initial astonishment. 'Who's the lucky woman?'

'You'll have to wait for that information, I'm afraid. I'm having a little difficulty convincing her that she is lucky.'

They clearly didn't believe this. No wonder he's conceited, Clary thought viciously, knowing that she was wrong, that his arrogance was the result of a naturally commanding personality with the strength and authority to back it up. Amid a chorus of teasing remarks about this incredibly blind and deaf, not to mention invisible love of his, remarks he parried with wit and good humour, they moved out on to a courtyard sheltered by the wings of the house.

'I know the sea is only ten minutes down the cliff,' Fay admitted as she caught Clary eyeing the swimming and spa pools with astonishment, 'but the path down is steep, and the sea is always much cooler than the pool. We like our creature comforts.'

'Sybarites.' That was Morgan, affectionately mocking.

Fay grinned at him. 'Oh, we all know you swim in icy-cold bush pools, but even you, iron man, have the pool at the homestead heated. Do sit down, Clary. Have you shown Clary your own very private pool yet, Morgan?'

'Not yet,' he said lazily, joining Clary on a wide, brilliantly patterned sofa.

He kept his eyes on Fay; she was smiling at him as though she had discerned a secret. Perhaps she had but no sign of it appeared in her voice as she said, 'You must. It's so beautiful, a pool on a wide ledge halfway down the big hill behind the homestead. It's surrounded by bush and it has a waterfall feeding it and about a hundred feet of rapids at the outlet.'

'Down quite a steep cliff covered with trees and thick with rocks.' Sam Oxten smiled reminiscently at his wife. 'Up which I had to push you, if I remember correctly. I know Morgan refused to help.'

The two Oxtens and Morgan exchanged smiles. Karen demanded, 'Where is this pool? Why haven't I been shown it? Morgan, you've been holding out on me.'

'It's difficult to get to,' Morgan said coolly.

'The only reason we went is that Morgan told Fay he'd learned to swim in it and she's insatiably curious.'

Sam winked at Clary. 'And when we got there—at last!—nothing would induce her to even dip a toe in it.'

'I should think not! It looked freezing!' Fay was laughingly indignant, wrinkling her nose at her husband's mockery. 'And I wanted to go up because Morgan said there were native orchids in the bush there. It is so lovely, with a huge *titoki* tree on a grassy bank which has a long rope suspended from a branch so anyone who's brave enough to swim can swing right out over the pool and drop into it from a great height!'

She shuddered; Clary's eyes met Morgan's amused, uncommunicative gaze and she knew who that rope was for. He used the pool at the homestead to keep fit, swimming lengths for over half an hour each day. Now she wondered how often he climbed the cliff to that other pool and used the rope as he had when he was a reckless daredevil of a boy.

The conversation drifted, became a discussion on an exhibition at the Art Gallery in Auckland, a selection from the Queen's collection of da Vinci nature drawings, including the superb 'Deluge' series.

Clary listened silently to the comments and observations. Karen was enthusiastic but not knowledgeable, the others spoke with understanding and delight. From art the conversation moved on to sailing and some mild gossip, thence to a projected visit by one of the great English ballet companies, the best way to deal with an entire smoked marlin, and a new potter Fay had discovered.

'She's marvellous!' she assured them all fervently. 'Her work has a lovely sculptural quality, and she's done some fantastic things with glazes. I bought one of her bowls which is a symphony, a poem; as miraculous as a sunset!'

Karen teased her about her enthusiasm, but Morgan asked the name of the potter.

'Yes, I thought you'd be interested. She's Jennet Hollingworth.'

'Rafe Hollingworth's wife?' This did interest Karen. 'That's her. You know Rafe, don't you, Morgan? Weren't you and he at school together? He's an absolute dish with a fabulous station up north. Jennet was his step-sister. She was an actress in Australia before she came home and married him. Melissa Addison is her half-sister.

'Trent's wife?' Karen leaned forward, her expression alert and, as her glance touched Clary's face, just a little smug. It was as if she was staking her claim to inhabit a circumscribed, exclusive little world. She gave an artificial laugh and rolled her eyes heavenwards. 'Oh, but Trent is a gorgeous man, a real brigand. We all went into shock when he married the first time.'

Morgan must have noticed that taunting little glance, for he calmly told them what all but Clary must have known. 'He started off in electronics—he's quite brilliant in that field. Eventually he gained control of the Durrant group and pulled it out of the red. His first wife is Sir Peter Durrant's granddaughter.'

'That marriage was a very odd business.' But Karen met with no encouragement to expand and finished lamely, 'I wonder what happened to her. Last I heard she was in London . . .'

They were off again, chatting about people most of whom were just names to Clary although occasionally she recognised one which turned up in the news, sometimes in the financial section, as often in reviews of art or books. Between them they seemed to know everyone of any importance in the country. Apart from Karen they were not trying to make Clary feel inadequate; the conversation was light and amusing, but if anything was needed to hammer home the difference between their life-styles and hers, it was this idle way of pleasantly filling in an idle afternoon.

Apparently content to sit and listen, Morgan said

very little, occasionally dropping in an explanatory remark or lifting a brow at some of Karen's more outrageous gossip. Clary watched the ice melt in her drink, a delicious concoction of fruit juice and white rum, and pondered on the peculiar differences between the class system in New Zealand and that of Britain. And all the while she was conscious of every breath the man beside her took, the slight movements of that magnificent body, her attention focused on him in a way which almost excluded the others.

More guests came to dinner, pleasant people who laughed and flirted and ate the delicious food and drank Sam's drinks with enthusiasm. Clary enjoyed herself. She was not beautiful like Karen, nor exuberant and funny like the only other unattached girl, who on arrival had cast herself into Morgan's arms and kissed him with considerable vivacity, but she could conduct a mild flirtation as well as the next woman, and hold her end up in an intelligent conversation.

She was well looked after. Fay was an excellent hostess, always alert to see that none of her guests felt neglected, and Tony hovered, flirting and flattering. The few times when she could have felt a little alone, Morgan was soon beside her; clearly he was watching. She felt protected, a sensation as unusual as it was pleasant.

While all this happened the sun set slowly in a regal display of golds and scarlets. With its departure a cool little breeze sprang up.

'Cold?' asked the man with whom she had been discussing the possibility that protea flowers would be the country's next big horticultural breakthrough. He spoke quickly, the words blurring together. 'I'll warm you.'

Hemmed in between a slatted screen and an oleander in a large tub, Clary was unable to avoid the arms which suddenly groped for her. Belatedly she realised that he had had just enough to drink to turn his mind from thoughts of exports to flirtation. A pity. He'd been quite interesting to talk to.

She said pleasantly, 'If you'll let me by I'll get something warmer to wear.'

'I'll keep you warm,' he said obstinately, his mouth searching greedily across her cheek.

'I'm afraid I don't want you to,' she retorted, standing stiff and unresponsive in his grasp. 'In fact, if you don't let me go I'll be forced to knee you in the groin. And while you're rolling around in agony I'll explain to everyone why I did it.'

The icy distaste in her voice finally got through. He dropped his arms and stepped back, peering owlishly at her. 'No need to do that,' he said warily, backing further away.

No, not a nasty man, merely one who turned amorous when he'd had a little too much to drink.

'Dean, your wife is looking for you.' Morgan made no attempt to hide the steel in his level voice. He loomed up behind the hapless Dean, who gave him a startled look, muttered something and headed, none too steadily, back to the rest of the party.

'Thanks.' Clary was warmed by the realisation that he had come looking for her.

'Think nothing of it.' The steel was naked and cutting. 'You coped admirably, but do try not to be manoeuvred into any more corners. Tony is waiting for the same opportunity.'

He was *furious*. Clary flinched and put out a tentative hand to touch his forearm. Beneath her fingers the muscles were rigid with tension. Unwittingly she stroked across the firm warm skin and his other hand came over and covered hers. Only then did she look up into his face. He was frightening, the skin drawn over its beautifully moulded framework, his eyes blazing gold.

'I don't like to see anyone touch you,' he said

tonelessly. 'It hurts me. I've known Dean for years—
he's a nice chap—hell, even his wife laughs at his
amorous tendencies—but I could have killed him then.
Come on, it's almost time we left.'

Shaken as much by the leap of her pulses as by the
realisation that she had escaped only narrowly from
danger, she went back with him to where the lights
bloomed and people provided a measure of safety.

'Ah, there you are.' Fay gave them a shrewd look
before smiling beguilingly at Morgan. 'If you'll
relinquish Clary to me I'll show her that piece by
Jennet Hollingworth. I keep it in my bedroom where I
can gloat over it.'

'Off you go, Clary.'

Morgan's voice was smooth but Clary took a deep
breath before following the older woman into the
house.

'He's an overpowering man, isn't he?' Fay remarked
lightly, ending on a questioning note so faint that
Clary probably imagined it.

'He's angry with me. I got bailed up by Dean
Somebody-or-other and Morgan arrived on the scene
as I was disentangling myself.' There, that should
convince Fay that nothing had happened. Morgan
would be furious if she caused gossip; she had noticed
his distaste at some of Karen's wilder flights.

'Oh dear, Dean is a nuisance! I'm so sorry. One
thing, he's easy enough to choke off.'

'It was hardly discreet of me.' Clary's voice was wry.

'My dear, you weren't to know. Morgan is not such
a chauvinist as to believe that you encouraged Dean,
he knows him. He was probably cross with him for
harassing you. There, what do you think of my bowl?'

It was a superb thing, the pottery almost as thin as
porcelain, with a red-gold glaze which held all the
depth and fire of a volcano.

'Go on, touch it,' Fay urged, and watched with a
satisfied smile as Clary caressed the lovely thing.

After some minutes of admiration Fay led the way back to the terrace. They arrived just in time to see the vivacious little blonde who had embraced Morgan so ardently when she arrived launch herself on to his knee and cover his smiling face with kisses before pressing her mouth to his.

A chorus of whistles and light-hearted jokes greeted this display. Morgan's lean hands came up and grasped the girl about the waist before, revealing incredible strength, he stood up with her and set her lightly on her feet.

A primitive, shattering jealousy held Clary in stasis. Ignoring Fay's amused comment, she had to force herself to bend as though she had caught something in her sandal; when she straightened Morgan was smiling down into the blonde's pouting little face before he turned her away with a pat on the shoulder and a remark which made those around roar with more laughter. The blonde swung back and shook her fist at him, but she was laughing, too, leaning for a moment into him with a familiarity which spoke of more than friendship.

Recalled to her duty as hostess Fay said, 'Oh, that Vicky! You can't help liking her, even though she gets away with murder. Probably that's why she gets away with murder. You need another drink, Clary. Let's see what Sam can produce,' but Clary didn't follow her. Here, in the semi-gloom of the eaves, she was safe from observation. Out there the lights were bright enough to reveal Karen's face, naked in its misery, all beauty fled.

Morgan replied to his petite companion's comments with another devastating smile and a kiss on the cheek before he turned and without looking her way made his way to where Clary stood half-hidden, her whole being locked in a rigor of desolation.

'Don't eat me with your eyes,' he said, his sardonic glance missing nothing, 'or people will begin to wonder if you're not more than my mother's nurse.'

'And that would never do, would it? I should imagine they're probably wondering why your mother's nurse isn't with your mother.'

The cold words were heavy with self-contempt. The sight of Karen's unhappiness had forced her to realise just what she was courting if she allowed him to bulldoze her into loving him. Disillusionment and pain; exactly what Angus was suffering for daring to love where wisdom failed him. Move out of the circle of your own experience and you deserve what you get, she told herself, holding her face averted from his penetrating gaze.

'You look like a Fury,' he said deliberately, 'beautiful and terrifying and stony-hearted. My friends are not so unreasonable that they will think there's anything odd about even the most dedicated nurse taking an occasional afternoon off.'

'And of course they are accustomed to seeing you with a woman in tow. In fact, they'd think it strange if the irresistible Morgan Caird——'

'If you want a fight I'll indulge you in the car. Until then, curb your tongue—or I'll do it for you. And then everyone *will* have something to talk about.'

The threat was no less effective for being delivered in a cool, almost indifferent voice. Clary swallowed to ease the obstruction in her throat before obeying the economical gesture of one lean hand which propelled her towards their host and hostess.

Ten minutes later they were on the road back to the Valley, the snarl of the Ferrari echoing Clary's emotions. Rebelliously she stared through the windscreen as the headlights cut a shocking swathe through the swift-falling darkness, pinpointing various creatures of the night, a hedgehog, the startled flight of some small bird in front of them.

Almost immediately they abandoned the tarseal of the main highway, turning inland along one of the back-country roads. The powerful engine made short work of the steep gradients as they wound through hills and along a narrow valley. Against her will Clary found herself admiring Morgan's driving. He seemed to know by instinct how to get the big car without fuss or drama around tight corners and through the drifts of gravel which could have made the road dangerous.

'When I was in Italy,' she said quietly, 'I drove some friends across the mountains in the north. We came to a rather hair-raising section and halfway up a mountain discovered that bits of the road had slipped away, leaving a one-way stretch with no edge. It looked as though the other half of the road could go any minute.'

'And?'

'And the van was pretty shot, we didn't know if it would ever get to the top if we stopped. There was no room to turn around in and it was pouring with rain. I was terrified.' She gave a small sigh, remembering just how frightened and lacking in confidence she had been. 'Not as terrified as the others, though. The boys bit their tongues trying to give me advice without flustering me and Donna had her eyes shut all the way. You remember Donna, she was with me——'

'I remember her,' he said with finality. 'Are you such a bad driver?'

'No, I'm a good driver, but both men were convinced that a woman is automatically inferior to almost any man when it comes to driving. Or most things,' she finished, remembering them.

'They sound very young.'

'A little older than I was.'

'How long were you together?'

She shrugged, uneasy at a metallic undertone to the question. 'Three months. Not nearly long enough to see everything I wanted to see in Europe, but at least I knew the places I wanted to go back to.'

Tension seeped from her bones as he began to talk of various places he had visited in Europe; once more she was surprised at how easy it was to talk to him. He had a dry, almost cynical attitude which should have repelled her yet beneath it she discerned an essential humanity. He spoke warmly, respectfully, of a farming family in Greece, admiring their tough pragmatism and the kindness which went with it, then told her a hilarious anecdote of a meal in a small cliff town in France where the cook had wept into the soup and confided his marital troubles in language which was rich and Rabelaisian, as salty as his tears and the soup.

Clary astonished herself by giggling, before capping it with the time she had been kissed on the neck by an amorous Italian waiter in one of the most famous cafés in Rome.

'And what did your boyfriend think of that?'

A note of—coolness? contempt?—in his voice sobered her. Rather stiffly she returned, 'The boys laughed, of course. What do you think they should have done? Hit him?' She invested the last word with a delicate scorn which should have made him feel like the barbarian he was.

'I would have.'

Flat and dangerous, the observation sent a cold thread crawling up her spine. She turned her head to scan his profile, cruel in its aquiline strength against the pale backglow of the lights. It was probably useless to try to explain but she did it just the same.

'It was purely light-hearted. He was a real tease. It was sheer high spirits on his part. And neither of the boys had any right to object. We were travelling companions, no more. For mutual protection. Oh, what's the use!'

'None. None at all. My mother tells me that I've been possessive since before I could say, "Mine!" I don't share, especially not my women.'

'But I am not one of your women!'

'No. You are the woman. And there's nothing I can do about it.' Incredibly, he laughed, although there was no humour in the sound. 'Shattering. If I'd been warned that I'd fall victim to love at first sight I'd have scoffed to high heaven. Then it happened, just like that. One look, and I knew we belonged together. I'd finally found my woman.'

'Love?' she asked smoothly, fiercely, repressing an atavistic thrill at such a blatant statement of ownership. '*Love*, Morgan?'

'Call it what you like, it exists.'

'I call it lust,' she bit out. 'Concupiscence, lechery, carnality, greed. That's what it is. The blind urge to reproduce, if you want to be polite about it. What——?'

The car slid to a halt. As the note of the engine died Clary stared around, realising that they were stopped in a wide area sheltered from view of the road by an enormous heap of gravel.

'They're going to straighten and realign the road,' Morgan told her conversationally as the lights flicked off. 'That's why this convenient stockpile of metal.'

The click of the seat-belt clip resounded in the silence. Now that her sight was attuned to moonlight Clary could see the harsh purpose which hardened his features.

Nervously she asked, 'Why have we stopped?'

'Oh, Clary,' he mocked, unclipping her belt with a swift sure movement.

She grabbed at the strap as it moved past her body. 'I warn you, if you think you can——'

'Darling, I'm just going to clear up a misconception or two,' he said as he opened the door. 'I think honesty in a relationship is vital, don't you?'

Sarcasm sharpened the words into an unanswerable statement. Biting her lip, she wondered what on earth he was going to do, watching suspiciously as he swung around the front of the car. When he opened her door she protested, but he gently extracted her from her seat and draped his arm about her shoulder.

'Uncomfortable things, cars,' he observed. 'Still, beggars can't be choosers.'

'You promised you wouldn't touch me.' It was futile to struggle against that rawhide strength but she did. He merely tightened his grip, being careful not to hurt her.

'Clearly I can't be trusted.' He was mocking her, the even, taunting words breathed into her ear as he bent to open the rear door. 'I think a demonstration is the only way to prove that you're wrong.'

He foiled her attempt to escape by sliding into the car first and pulling her in after him. She ducked to avoid the roof and ended up in his lap in a tangle of arms and legs and anger, and a slow deep excitement which came from the depths of her soul.

'This,' he said deliberately, pulling her head back with a cruel hand in her hair, 'is lechery. Take note, or I might find it necessary to repeat the lesson.'

What followed was a calculated humiliation. Even as his mouth crushed hers, forcing it to open to a crude, suffocating invasion, his free hand slid the silken length of her thigh, hesitated long enough for her to flinch, and then moved to her breast, finding with accuracy the aroused tip. Clary writhed in shame, hating him, hating the reckless treachery of her body which responded even to this callous subjugation. Desperately she struck at him. More by luck than aim her open hand connected noisily with his cheek.

He lifted his head, surveying her furious face with glittering eyes. He smiled, a slow, dangerous curving of that ruthless mouth.

'Do you like to receive pain as well as inflict it, my lovely?'

Strong white teeth closed, not gently, on her throat for a second before moving to hover above the full curve of her breast.

'You dare,' she breathed, a cold fear beginning to replace anger.

Again he smiled. Lean fingers roughly flicked free the pewter buttons of her dress, quelled her renewed struggles with a ruthless economy of movement which forced a breathless whimper from her. His remorseless hand wrenched at fragile lace and her bra fell agape.

'You've ruined it!' she spat, hiding her fear behind clenched teeth.

'Ah, lechery enjoys destruction.' Beneath the thick screen of his lashes blazed a cynical appreciation which was an insult in itself.

On her exposed skin his breath was warm and potent but the mouth which fastened on to the shadowed bud of her breast was heated and avid and her anger fled, lost in sensual submission.

'Don't,' she whispered, hot tears blinding her eyes when at last she lay quiescent in the hard prison of his arms.

'Why not?' The words were slurred, but the predatory note in them made her feel sick. Heat stung her skin, became transmuted into an icy lethargy as his hand swept from the high warm peak of her breast to settle threateningly on her thigh.

'Why not?' he repeated. 'Lust takes no notice of pleading, or prayers for mercy. Lust says the devil take you and your needs, your desires. Why should I stop, Clary? Why should you expect me to stop? If this is mere carnality you should know not to expect anything more from me than my own self-gratification.'

She bit her lip, determined not to give him the admission he was trying to wring from her.

'Desire, now, desire is different. Desire encompasses consideration,' he murmured, and the cruel hands gentled, caressing her skin with loving care. 'Desire can be gentle or fierce but it is always tender. Desire is between two people ... desire is for lovers ...'

CHAPTER SEVEN

His voice wooed her. With gentle ardour he kissed the pale satin of her throat and a certain spot where her jaw met her ear. He was not rough but he was persistent, and the knowledgeable expertise of his love-making made her shiver, and turn her face into the hard wall of his chest in complete surrender.

'Desire is sensitive,' that disturbing voice continued, 'and exciting . . . Desire gives as well as takes . . .'

Clary groaned as his mouth inscribed slow, lazy circles over the smooth skin he had bared so violently only minutes before. The soft friction of his cheek on her flushed skin was unbearably stimulating; she rested her chin against the textured warmth of his hair, inhaling the faint natural scent of him with trembling delight. Shudders of exquisite pleasure ran through as his mouth found its goal. The soft, tugging sensation seemed to sear through her body, almost more anguish than rapture. Her hand curled against the lean jaw, her palm and fingers appreciating the tiny movements of the muscles he used in this delicious torture.

A strange inertia weighted her limbs. A soft little moan caught in her throat and her burning, shaking hand quested down the strong line of his neck to its juncture with his shoulder. Beneath her fingers the tendons were strung taut as wires; emboldened by the deep, rasping breath which lifted his chest she explored its width, finding through the fine tangle of hair and heated skin that every muscle was flexed and tense.

And all the while she imbibed his fragrance and learned the contours of his torso his mouth pleasured her until she flamed for him, their mutual passion igniting a blaze which forced stumbling, unheard words from her tongue.

'Morgan,' she whispered. 'Oh, God, Morgan . . . I want—please . . .'

A rigor shook her. She responded to the burning frustration the only way she could, arching her body in a provocative, involuntary movement, every cell screaming for fulfilment, aching and acceptant.

His dark head lifted and he kissed the mouth which opened in sensual invitation to him, penetrating the sweet depths in a blatant evocation of another more powerful and fundamental penetration.

For long moments they strained together like lovers on the brink of the abyss. Then he dragged his mouth from hers and held her with tormenting gentleness, his trembling lips against her temple, until the violent thudding of their hearts eased and reality began to douse the conflagration his expert seduction had ignited. At last, his ragged tones revealing just how much control he was being forced to exert, he said, 'And desire can be restrained. It is not greedy, it is not frightening.'

Clary could have wailed her frustration to the peeping moon. Instead, she drew a hiccuping breath and with a control which matched his, muttered into his shoulder, 'What do you want, for heaven's sake?'

'I've told you. Everything.'

'I'll give you everything,' she whispered through a fog of unsatisfied passion. 'Now, if you want it. Why are you torturing me like this?'

He gave a curious breathy laugh. 'It's not just you who is suffering. Can't you feel how I hurt?'

'Why? You could have taken me.' It humiliated her to admit it yet it was stupid to pretend. His lovemaking revealed his experience; he knew exactly what he had done to her, and how easily.

'I gave up making love in cars years ago,' he said,

the words threaded with the same irony which muted his smile.

'You're asking the impossible,' she said dully. 'I shouldn't even be living in your house. Angus is too dangerously close to the edge for me to do anything that might push him over. I won't have an affair with you—sooner or later he would find out. You might just as well try to persuade me to marry you!'

'Marriage is irrelevant.' He scanned her defeated expression closely. His face was etched with a kind of stern remoteness which was so unlike his usual confident sophistication that she felt she was talking to a stranger.

Not for anything would she have admitted that she winced. 'I know. It's just as irrelevant as an affair.'

He pulled the gaping lapels of her dress together, lingering a moment to cup the warm weight of her breast.

'What is relevant,' he said quietly, 'is your fear of losing control. Why, darling?'

She sat up and with shaking hands fastened the buttons over the remnants of her bra. Gravely he watched her, making no further attempt to touch her but when she was once more covered he pulled her back into the haven of his arms. The tightly wound tension in him was communicated to her. She was afraid of this weakness in her; she could deal better with the mindless world of passion he made for them than this dangerous gentleness. She summoned up an image of Susan, her beautiful face dazed with pleasure as she lay with him in ecstasy, Susan who probably still recalled with sensual enjoyment the hours she had spent in his bed.

Clary's teeth clamped on to her lower lip. She fought to banish the picture of them clasped together in voluptuous delight. It made her feel sick and angry and betrayed.

Perhaps that was better than feeling frightened. She

had thought that Morgan's threat to her was purely physical, that she was endangered only by the flaming incandescence of their sexual need for each other, but his last comment was altogether too perceptive. She huddled still, feeling the steady beat of his heart, and hoped that it was just a shot in the dark.

His next comments proved her wrong. 'You were afraid right from the start,' he pursued. 'I thought at first that it was because you had never felt such an attraction, and I was pleased, because I have never wanted a woman as I want you. But it wasn't entirely that, was it? You were—you are afraid of the emotion itself, not just of me. What made you decide that men could only hurt you, Clary?'

Why not tell him? It was easier to give in than continue resisting. In a voice that held no emotion she said, 'In our family we don't fall in love, we run to obsessions. When I was seventeen my father became besotted with a girl about three years older than me. He left us and went to live with her.'

'That was tough, but it happens.' The wide shoulders lifted in a shrug. 'It happens all the time. The Americans call it a mid-life crisis.'

'Is that what it was? It killed my father. She was a bitch. She lived with him for a year and in that year she went through every cent he had. He even sold the house, put my mother out on to the street.' She choked back a sob. 'Not quite literally, but she had to find a flat, and a job. I was at boarding school but there was no money for me to finish there. When his lover had gone through his money she left Dad for another, richer man. He had nowhere to go, so he came back to us and sat down and willed himself to die.'

He made no reply and she looked up into the stark perfection of his features, limned by moonglow. Harshly, so quickly that she stumbled over the words she finished, 'He couldn't face life without her. We had to watch as he deliberately killed himself.'

'And do you think the same thing might happen to Angus?' He spoke in formal, even tones, revealing nothing.

'I don't know.' She was appalled at having her most secret fears put so bluntly into words. Nervously she ran her tongue over her top lip. 'He worshipped Susan and she took all that he had and flung it back in his face. She said—she s-said——'

He held her closely while she wept out her anger and fear, making no attempt to comfort her until she choked into a silence broken only by the involuntary sobs of over-indulgence. Then he tilted her face and wiped it with his handkerchief and kissed her brow and her wet eyes.

'My poor little love,' he said very gently. 'All that worry and fear! For what it's worth I think you've underestimated both the depth of your brother's feelings for Susan and his powers of recuperation. I happen to believe that love is only love when it's reciprocal. And Susan didn't love Angus, so whatever he felt for her, intense though it might have been, was not love. No, I know you won't believe me, but do believe that he's over the worst. The front man who deals with him is quite relieved because he no longer looks and behaves as though he's heading for a nervous breakdown. As for your father——' he paused, before ending calmly, '—I think your father died of pride.'

'*Pride?*' She reacted fiercely, sitting up with a swift movement which catapulted her from his embrace on to the seat beside him. 'He had no pride left!'

'Exactly.' Morgan stilled her twisting hands in his warm, firm clasp. 'She hit him in his pride, made him look a fool, and he couldn't cope with it. Never underestimate the power of pride, Clary. It's killed as many people as sex or greed. He died because he wasn't strong enough to face a world which found him ridiculous. Angus is not so passive.'

He looked down into her astonished face and gave a tight smile. 'I'm looking forward to meeting your mother. I presume that's who you and your brother take after. Because you aren't weak, Clary, you're like spider's silk, fine and clear and strong as steel. In your innermost heart you don't class Angus with your father, either. I can hear the pity in your voice when you speak of your father, but there is no taint of it when you mention Angus.'

She could not respond but as they drove home in a silence which held an oddly peaceful wordless communion she wondered whether Morgan could possibly be correct in his assessment of her father. And she hugged the memory of his kindness, so unexpected, yet not out of character. He had the gentleness of the strong.

Slowly, in that silent drive, she realised that what she felt for him must be love.

Just like that, she mused later as she made herself ready for bed, going mindlessly through the familiar rituals. She had looked across an English field and fallen in love, deeply, irrevocably—hopelessly. For although he had spoken optimistically of Angus he must know, as she did, that no man would be able to bear his sister marrying the man who had, however innocently, seduced his wife away from him.

If seduction could ever be called innocent.

It's not *fair*! she thought, too anguished to appreciate how inappropriate the childhood lament was. Why had it been Susan who was so alluring that the two men Clary loved had wanted her?

Not that it really mattered. Pride and her moral code—and Clary's sense of self-preservation—would not permit the complete capitulation Morgan needed. He might say now that he had never felt this way before, but was it a difference in degree or one in kind? And if—*when*—he lost interest in her there would be absolutely nothing she could do about it. It would be agony, and she would have no right to feel this savage sense of possession.

It was then that she realised how much she had allowed herself to be seduced into hoping that perhaps this time, this emotion he felt for her might be different, that it might last.

'Oh, you fool!' she whispered to her angry reflection. 'You great idiot!'

And watched as all colour fled from her pale skin, leaving the freckles standing out like blotches beneath eyes almost black with mocking self-derision.

Resistance had not been enough. Whatever happened now, Morgan had marked her for life. If she held out against him she would always be eaten by the savage frustration of unsatisfied desire. And she would hunger for him until the day she died ...

Perhaps the idea was born then, fretting at the edge of her conscious mind, teasing, elusive. Perhaps it burgeoned in the following week which Morgan spent mostly in Auckland, not arriving home until late, twice staying the night in his apartment.

Not that the idea ever emerged full-blown into her head. By the time she had to admit its existence she realised that she had been subconsciously examining it for some time.

The process of making a decision was not easy. To start off with, the idea ran directly counter to the way she had run her life. Always, it seemed, she had been afraid of emotion, obsessed with a kind of terror at the power it could unleash. She had built defences and crouched behind them. Not even her family had been allowed too close. She had told Morgan they were not demonstrative and it was true, but in her case a fundamental fear of being hurt intensified a natural reserve.

But pain had come. Pain caused by the bitter treachery of body and heart. It was with the only unbiased part of her that she assessed her idea and it was her mind which finally gave her permission.

Looked at logically, there was no reason why she should not take Morgan for her lover. All of the reasons she had given him were the products of her fears. When the passion between them burnt out she could go on her way, scarred perhaps, but not maimed for life. He wanted her submission. Very well then, he should have it. The leopard could not change his spots, so it was unfair to expect him to be otherwise than he was, a man of powerful magnetism, having a connoisseur's appreciation of women.

And remembering more of Susan's remarks Clary smiled with painful cynicism and told herself that at least she would have memories to feed her hungry heart—told herself all the lies which gave a gloss of respectability to her decision to seduce him.

It should not prove too difficult, this seduction ploy, even for a woman as completely inexperienced as she was. Recalling how the electricity had arced through him when she touched him, she smiled a sultry woman's smile which would have shocked her had she been able to see it.

Perhaps the struggle her decision caused her showed. After a long night her employer looked sharply at her and asked, 'Are you sickening for something?'

'No. I didn't sleep well.'

Mrs Hargreaves appeared to accept the evasion. 'Feel like driving the car?'

'Yes, of course.'

So with Ruth they drove out to the coast and there Mrs Hargreaves bought an old, dilapidated Victorian villa which she clearly couldn't wait to get into and redecorate. It was, she announced to an equally enthusiastic Ruth, the perfect place for grandchildren.

Once more Morgan didn't come home that evening. After dinner Clary found herself roaming about the garden, quite blind to the pictures Mrs Hargreaves had created there. She was filled with an intolerable restlessness, a corroding hunger which ate into the fabric of her composure until she was almost distraught. She knew what it was, of course.

In a gesture as graceful as it was unforced, she looped an arm around the trunk of an Australian frangipani and cooled her hot cheek against its bark while the sweet-spicy perfume of the yellow flowers gave tangible expression to her erotic yearnings.

'Oh hell,' she muttered furiously and strode back inside to meet a somewhat agitated Ruth just inside the door.

'Clary, I think you'd better take a look at her.' Ruth indicated the stairs with her head. 'She's excited——'

'Ruth, between you and me and the newel post, I'd say that I'm more likely to succumb to over-excitement than Mrs Hargreaves.' Clary gave her a conspiratorial grin. 'A charge of dynamite might just manage to carry her off, but I'd lay odds on her even then. Are you really worried? You know her better than anyone except Morgan.'

'Better than he does, too.' But the worry had eased from the housekeeper's expression. 'Yes, I know I fuss, and I'm not really concerned, but I would feel better if you checked her out. She's up there drawing plans!'

'Why did she decide to buy a new house? I thought she loved the Valley.'

With a somewhat astonished look which made Clary flinch Ruth said, 'Well, Morgan is going to marry sooner or later, and the Valley is his home. The flat in Auckland is lovely and big, but it's no place to bring up a family, and his mother knows perfectly well that no bride is going to take kindly to a resident mother-in-law. Besides, she just loves doing places up, she'd have made a superb decorator, but there's nothing left for her to do here. Oh, the new place will give her a wonderful new lease of life.'

There was no doubt about that. Up in her bedroom

Mrs Hargreaves was making notations all over the surveyor's report. When she looked up she gave Clary a smile which revealed that she knew exactly why she was there.

'Ruth's an old fusspot,' she declared. 'I haven't felt as good as this for years.'

'Well, perhaps not, but it might be a good idea if you went to bed a bit earlier than usual.'

'And what about you? Feeling restless, are you? I saw you flitting about in the garden. Why don't you go for a walk?'

'Oh, I'll stick around——'

'In case I die of excitement? You can't possibly devote yourself to me night and day. It's not sensible!'

'I was employed——'

'Oh, rubbish!' Mrs Hargreaves looked as though she would have preferred to use a stronger term but she went on reasonably enough, 'Now, tell me the truth, is there any reason to suspect that I might be struck down tonight or any other night by another heart attack?'

'Well—of course not. You know your doctor is very pleased with your progress.'

'Of course I do. I'm not an idiot. But you are starting to act like one. I told you once before that I'm waiting for my grandchildren, but that's not the only reason I'm living, believe me! If it will make you happier, Ruth can stay with me until you get back. Now go away, you're as restless as a dog in a thunderstorm; it's bad for me to have to watch you prowl about as if the end of the world is just around the corner. Go on, away you go!'

Clary laughed and risked a quick kiss on her patient's cheek, much to their mutual astonishment. 'Oh, very well, then. Just don't you do anything energetic,' she warned, tossing over her shoulder, 'or get too excited over Ruth's scandal!'

Her nurse's instinct told her she had no need to

worry over her patient but once through the door Clary hesitated, her expression almost haunted. She clasped her hands between her breasts in a vain attempt to still the rapid beating of her heart; her skin was over-sensitive, reacting too violently to the oppressive heaviness of the atmosphere.

It should have denoted the approach of an electrical storm, but although the sky was filmed by cloud there was no sign of any thunderheads. The sultry sunlight was smoke-orange in shade, reminding her that there had been bushfires in Australia. This must be the smoke from them, carried thousands of miles across the Tasman Sea by the westerlies of the past week. Fortunately this time no one had died in the fires but she felt immeasurably sad as she thought of the destruction and the wreckage of people's lives left in their wake.

Wearily she made her way to her bedroom. Perhaps she should just go to bed. Discarding the idea even as it was born, she made a sudden decision, changing into a pair of stout shoes. She met Ruth halfway up the stairs and told her that she was going up the valley to the pool. Morgan had not had time to take her there, but he had pointed out its location and she was confident that she could find it.

'You'll get hot and sticky,' Ruth told her prosaically. 'Still, if you've got excess energy to burn off it's as a good a way as any, I suppose. Better take a torch.'

She did get hot and sticky, but the scramble up the steep face gave her tension something to feed on, dissipating its strength by substituting hard exertion for foreboding.

By the time she reached the top it was dusk and she was almost exhausted. From beneath the *titoki* tree she watched a sunset as dramatic as any she had seen in all her wanderings, an inferno of crimson and scarlet and hot oranges and pinks, fading at last behind the dim veils of night. Before the magnificent spectacle vanished the moon arose behind her, an enormous globe like a muted, mysterious sun. The air became marginally cooler but it was the stifling burden of the atmosphere which caused Clary to shiver. The pool glimmered, beckoning, alluring. She removed her shoes, revelling in the cool softness of the grass against her hot feet. The little dell beneath the *titoki* tree was now a cup of shadow; she stood looking about her while tears stung her eyelids.

Angrily, scarcely aware of what she was doing, she put the torch down and began to tear at her clothes, freeing herself from their clammy embrace until she stood slim and naked in the strange hazy glow of the moon.

The rope Fay had spoken of dangled invitingly over the water. Clary ran up the steep little bluff and jumped, snatching at the rope with a ferocity which helped ease the tension coiled within her. Out she swung in a long arc over the water; at the furthest and highest point she let go and dived gracefully into the black pool. It welcomed her with the sensuous sweep of water about her heated body. Abruptly her head emerged into the forest-scented air in a spray of glittering droplets as she shook it to free the clinging curls of excess water. She swam rapidly back and forth, still driven by her demons, until something impelled her out. When she rose to step up on to the bank water streamed from her in veils of gold and silver, inextricably blended, shimmering the length of her lithe nakedness. Again she shook her head, then ran her hands from her breasts to her thighs in a gesture which was unconsciously provocative, hating the tight bands of tension which wound through every nerve and cell in her body.

CHAPTER EIGHT

'CLARY.'

Her initial shock of terror fled as soon as she recognised the speaker. Although all she could see was his silhouette, big, almost menacing as he waited by the tumbled heap of clothes, she recognised him. With the departure of fear came the resolution of that other tension which had plagued her. She smiled, and came out of the water like a naiad of old confronting the mortal she had chosen for her lover.

'Morgan,' she said and her intention was clear in her voice, her carriage, the explicit promise in her smile. She stopped in front of the tall, unmoving figure and raised her finger to outline his mouth, so intriguing with its blend of austerity and passion.

'I was waiting for you,' she whispered.

The last wary remnants of the cautious Clary of the past fled as she admitted that her only chance of freedom lay in the forbidden pleasure he represented. Eventually, when she was sated by a surfeit of carnality, she could leave him.

So she said his name again and the tip of her forefinger slid between the straight line of his lips and met the soft edge of his tongue. Frozen, she by shyness, they stood motionless. Then his tongue curled around her fingertip and she felt every nerve in her body blaze into excitement.

Nervously she jerked her hand free, lowering her glance to his chest. She began to undo the buttons of his shirt. She felt the harsh in-drawing of his breath but was not ready for the way his hand covered hers, trapping them against the warm, heavy beat of his heart.

'Are you sure?' he asked.

The thick, ragged note in his voice restored her confidence. Smiling again that blind primal smile, she nodded.

Still he hesitated, so she moved into him, leaning her gleaming, almost dry body against him in obedience to the prompting of age-old instincts. Her mouth found the tense line of his jaw and she whispered throaty little endearments until the potency of her feminine seduction broke his resistance.

He groaned as his arms enfolded her. For long moments his mouth crushed hers, giving no quarter, demanding submission. Clary gave it to him with a fierce driven hunger. After an aeon he lifted his head, muttering against her tender lips, 'I'm sorry, I'm sorry, I hurt you . . .'

Clary was totally given over to her long-repressed sensuality. The famished pressure of his kiss should have hurt, but if there had been pain it was lost in the seething tumult of sensations which surged through her.

What followed was erotic fantasy, a dream-like drama of passion and surrender played out beneath the eerie smoked orange of the moon. Laid down on to the sweet-smelling grass Clary was a slender white houri, possessed of knowledge gained by all the generations of women who had preceded her in love. With hands and mouth and throaty, smoky voice she adored the masculinity of the man she loved, and Morgan responded with such fevered skill that she was transported into another plane of existence. His touch roused trails of fire across her skin, igniting that other fire within her until she was aware of nothing else but the sensations which overwhelmed her, the scent of aroused masculinity, the sound of her heart as it tried to burst through the confines of her breast, the deep husky note of his voice when he whispered his appreciation of her offering.

And as she discovered the secrets of her body and

his, her heavy-lidded stare never wavered, noting the contrast of bronze skin against white, the dark colour which burned along his cheekbones, the incredibly erotic brush of his cheek against her breasts and the delicious savagery of his mouth around the tender aureoles which welcomed him so ardently.

Those primeval women who had been her forebears told her when to arch her back so that the length of her body pressed into the aroused strength of his, showed her how to circumvent his efforts to make their love-making a leisurely sophisticated affair. Here, beneath such a moon, he was on her territory, captive as she was of the age-old pulse of sexuality and the endless circle of birth and death, of life.

So Clary resisted his practised, civilised seduction with every bit of woman-magic she could call upon, and knew of her success when he groaned into her mouth and obeyed the demands of her body with the sudden, brutal invasion of his.

And that was right too, the pain and her acceptance of it, the melding of light and dark, strength and beauty, male and female, the sensual driving abandon until the ultimate ecstasy, the explosion of sensation which left them spent and trembling, all strength drained away.

It was right too that they sleep, bodies entwined beneath that glowing moon, beside that still pool; but only for a short time.

Clary woke gently, relaxed as never before. Her lashes flicked, then lifted and she was looking straight into the face of the man who had just taken her. She should have been appalled, disgusted with herself, shocked at her capacity for passion and the barbaric ferocity of their coming together. Instead, she felt an immense tenderness for him, and for her a kind of profound and lethargic smugness.

And a slow but unmistakable resurgence of the hunger which had precipitated all this. Tiny shivers of sensation heated her skin as his hand cupped her breast, testing the weight with possessive intimacy. He was smiling, the triumphant, rather astonished smile of a man who has been given more than he expected.

'I knew it would be incredible for us,' he said softly. 'I didn't realise just how incredible. As wild as a force of nature.'

'Sex is a force of nature.' She didn't begrudge him his triumph—was it not hers too?—so her voice entirely lacked tartness. It was, she decided dreamily, quite easy being a seductress. Tomorrow she might start to worry about things again, but tomorrow seemed a long way away.

In the meantime she lay sheltered in his strong embrace as his hands rediscovered the contours of her body. Soon, very soon, his dark profile would harden in the absorption of desire and that elemental fusion would happen again, and for a few minutes they would be freed by rapture from the confines of the world.

Lazily she turned her head so that she could press open-mouthed kisses into his shoulder, revelling in the rapid hoarseness of his breath, the way his muscles flexed in a sudden involuntary movement. It gave her an indescribable sense of power to be able to overset the controls of that clever brain, to make him as much a prisoner as she of the primordial forces hidden in them. His sophistication could not withstand the allure of her sensuality.

Suddenly his hand stopped that sensuous silky stroking.

'What the hell—?' he muttered, and turned her on to her back with an abrupt twist. Taken by surprise she rolled laxly, landing with a grimace.

'Blood,' he said harshly. 'You *bled*!'

She nodded unconcernedly. He was still staring at his hand. Slowly, as if he could not believe the evidence of his eyes, he reached out and touched the stain on her leg.

'You were a virgin.'

Again she nodded, smiling rather ironically at the gathering anger in his face.

'I don't suppose you've taken any precautions at all.'

Is that all that he was worried about? A thread of anger wove through her voice. 'Wrong. I'm on the pill.'

He closed his eyes briefly, perhaps in relief, and she decided not to tell him that her use of the pill was necessary because of the irritating irregularity which had used to bedevil her.

'OK,' he said between his teeth, 'but you were a virgin.'

Smiling, Clary lifted her arms to link them behind her head, knowing that this tightened and emphasised her breasts. She didn't want to discuss her virginity. She wanted him.

'Couldn't you tell?' she teased.

'What's the hell's got into you tonight? Lunacy?'

She sat up, turning towards him to run a provocative hand from his chest to his lean hip, her expression pensive. 'Oh, call it a return to the past,' she said lightly. 'A full moon, a virgin sacrifice, a ritual mating to ensure prosperity for the crops—we have all the ingredients.'

He made to speak but when she bent over him and kissed his mouth tenderly, his body shook. Lifting her head she smiled, sure of him once more, but he twisted away from her to his feet, and he was suddenly no man to be seduced for her pleasure but a menacing intruder in a moonlit idyll, man the aggressor, anger transmuting his lean grace into a threat.

Shivering, cold without him, Clary stared up at his averted face. 'What is it? What is the matter?' They were stupid questions, revealing the weakness which was the flaw in the fabric of her woman's power, especially when asked in a voice which quavered on the last word.

'For your information,' he gritted, leaning down to haul her to her feet, 'yes, I did realise that you were different, but as I've no experience with virgins I didn't recognise the proof of it. At that exact moment I wouldn't have cared if the world had shivered into nothingness around us.'

'Then what *is* the matter?' This time Clary demanded rather than asked, and there was no betraying break in her voice. 'Do you always snarl at your lovers after sex? If that's the case I'm surprised that you keep them.'

He replied harshly, 'No, I don't. And don't try to reduce this to the usual affair, either. We both know that this is something entirely new—for both of us.' When she didn't speak he finished angrily, 'I wish I knew what was going on in that lovely head of yours.'

'I don't see your problem. You've been trying to get me into your bed since you saw me. Well, you've done it. I think you should be pleased. Or else blasé. That's the usual course of events, surely?'

She had spoken coolly, but beneath the objective words there was provocation and she expected him to retaliate. Instead his hands tightened about hers and he said indistinctly, 'Nothing about you has followed the usual course of events. Oh, Clary . . .'

His mouth on hers was warm and searching. She sighed and relaxed against him, borne once more on the hot tide of passion which began to flow through them again. But Morgan tilted her face between his strong hands and scanned the dazed submission he saw there with unreadable eyes.

'When can you marry me?' he asked.

Clary's brain, already clouded by desire, went into a complete spin. She felt her mouth gape and closed it, swallowed and wished that she could break free of that shrewd, hard gaze.

'No, you hadn't given marriage a thought, had you? What did you have in mind for us, Clary? A *relationship*?' His voice invested the words with scornful contempt and his eyes seemed to bore into her soul. 'I'm not interested, thanks. I can't be content with a nice simple affair, quick and easy, still friends when it's over, no bones broken. I need more. I want you to marry me.' She shivered at the determination in his tone, and he said tersely, 'For God's sake, put your clothes back on.'

She obeyed, scrambling into the crushed garments with an icy anger which made her wrench them into place. When she looked up he was half dressed, his shirt slung over a tanned shoulder, his brows drawn into a frown.

'What happened tonight, Clary?' he asked quietly, the strange glow of the moon sliding over the strong angles and planes of his face. He looked magnificent, like a severe god, filled with power and authority.

Wearily Clary shook her head. 'It doesn't matter,' she said with a painful attempt at carelessness.

'Why, darling? A virgin as determined as you were doesn't throw all that self-imposed restraint to the winds on a whim. What happened?'

'Oh, blame the moon.'

Her flippancy made his lips tighten but that perceptive gaze still searched her face. 'Tell me, Clary,' he insisted.

'I gave in,' she flung at him. 'It's as simple as that. For once I decided to do what I wanted instead of the sensible thing. Is that so dreadful?'

'If it's the truth, no. Your sensuality is as much a part of you as your family loyalty and your intelligence, and that warmth you don't even know you have. And the way your eyes gleam with sly laughter when you make one of your appalling puns. But I don't think that was the entire reason, was it? Why did you give me everything I asked from you and then refuse to marry me?'

'You mentioned the family loyalty,' she retorted ally. 'If I married you I'd be betraying Angus.'

There was a taut silence. The moonlight spread its warm spell over the beautiful chiselled mask of his face, the strong neck and wide shoulders. Clary felt a clutch of sensation as her wanton brain recalled just how it had felt to have those shoulders block out the moon and the stars. Obstinately she repressed it. She had no regrets about what she had done, but such abandonment to passion was proving to be every bit as debilitating as she had suspected. Now all that she wanted to do was forget everything, Susan, Angus, her own turbulent thoughts, in the heated world of the senses into which he had initiated her. Why couldn't he accept what she was prepared to give so freely?

'If there were no Susan, no Angus, would you marry me?'

It was a loaded question but she faced it, and told him the truth. 'Probably, although with quite a few doubts.'

'What doubts?'

She shrugged, searching for the words. Finally she said, 'You keep telling me what you want, you need, like some emotional vampire. I don't hear much about *my* needs.'

He flung up his head as though she had hit him, and stared at her, his expression totally without emotion. She could not see through the thick fringe of his lashes to his thoughts; she did not know whether he understood what she was trying to get across to him.

At last he said in a shaken voice, 'I dare not. If you decide that you do not need me, do not want me, then I have to have face the fact that I will always be alone. I am a coward.'

She whispered his name and he said, 'No, I mean it. I have never needed a woman before. I don't know how to cope with it.' Incredibly he smiled, rueful and tender. 'I tried to rush you into some sort of commitment. I knew you thought I was the worst bastard unhung; I wanted you to change your mind and the only way I could do it was to keep you with me. So I blackmailed you into staying. I behaved like a fool, but I was desperate. And then I compounded my foolishness by trying to impress on you how much I needed you. I thought you might relax your guard a little. You have a compassionate heart.'

'Oh, Morgan!' She didn't know how to repond to his incredible admission. 'My dear, is that what you want from me? Compassion?'

'I'll take whatever I can get,' he said, suddenly confident, laughing, his teeth very white in the darkness. He caught her wrists and kissed her on the forehead then slid his arms around her in a shatteringly tender embrace.

Clary stiffened but the warmth of his body and the faint scent of him soothed her and she leaned her face into his throat, listening dreamily to the heavy regular beat of his pulse.

'The trouble with you,' he said into her ear, 'is that emotionally you're still seventeen. That was the year your father died, wasn't it?'

A kind of panic held her motionless. When she spoke it was barely audible. 'Yes.'

'After a year spent with his lover.'

She nodded and he said, 'I love the way your curls tickle. How did you feel about him, Clary? What were your emotions when you looked at him?'

Surprisingly she couldn't refuse him. 'At first I hated him. But he just *sat*, grey-faced and despairing, and died by inches, and all I could feel was pity and——'

'And?'

'And a kind of distaste.'

His mouth touched her fragile temple, warm and loving. 'And was that when you decided never to fall in love?'

She pushed at him but his grip was too tight. 'Don't you try psycho-analysing me like some cheap pop guru! Can't you accept that there is no future for us?'

'No,' he said implacably, 'I will not accept that. I have more respect for your brother than to believe that he would rather see you my mistress than my wife.'

'He'd be furious—and sick—if he knew that I was even staying here,' she hissed. 'He's not a sophisticated man of the world like you, swapping women with your friends and——'

'You had better stop right there,' he said icily.

She stopped. For a moment she had felt naked aggression in him, sensed the struggle he had to restrain it, and sighed, a tiny lost sound, when he regained control of his anger. 'I'm sorry,' she said in a small voice. 'That was below the belt.'

'And not true. I make no apologies for not living a celibate life before I met you, but my sexuality is satisfied by normal——'

'I know that,' she interrupted.

'Very well, then,' he said deliberately. 'Clary, I love you.'

Panic almost smothered her. 'I don't believe you,' she whispered, striving desperately for a steady voice. 'I won't marry you. Don't ask me.'

He laughed and kissed her, hard, and then as her mouth opened for him, with all the erotic mastery he possessed. When he lifted his head she was sighing, her body pressed ecstatically against his as her hands clenched on the smooth taut skin of his back.

'I'm not going to take you as my mistress,' he said deliberately into her throat. 'If you want this, you're going to have to marry me to get it.'

As she turned her face into the strength of his shoulder she smiled. Beneath her long lashes her eyes were slumbrous, the eyes of a confident temptress. This dark desire which held her captive bound him too in chains of sensuality. A short time ago she had experienced the power of her woman's body. He would be unable to resist her; she did not under-estimate the strength of his will but she knew now that willpower was little defence against a passion as intense as that which they generated.

The smile widened as he whispered mockingly into her ear, 'I'm going to enjoy it when you try to make me change my mind, darling.'

She bit into the salty skin, felt his answering shudder and looked up at him, her face mysterious and beckoning, a siren full of dangerous allure. His iron-clad assurance made her long to penetrate it, show him just how susceptible he was to her feminine fascination. He was so beautiful, she thought achingly, so perfect in every way. Not just physically, either. He intrigued her, he made her think and laugh—she wanted to know just how that cool, clever brain worked, it was a seduction in itself.

Why had he slept with Susan? Had she too gazed at him like this, still hungry for the superb sensations he wrung from her body? Yes, of course she had. How many other women had tasted the pleasure of paradise in his arms, experienced the strength and grace of his body, then wept when he went on his way? More than enough to give him that superb technique, she thought acidly, hating the visions of him shuddering with the same pleasure in Susan's arms, in the arms of a horde of beautiful women. But almost certainly not one of them had driven him beyond the bounds of that technique into the driving desperation to which he had succumbed in her arms.

Abruptly, wishing to hurt him, she said, 'I won't marry you, because it would kill Angus if I did,' and stepped away from him to turn towards the place where the track wound beside the rapids away from the pool.

He caught her up before she had gone more than a few steps; he had pulled his shirt back on and was doing up the buttons.

'I can see that he would dislike it at first,' he said logically, 'but he's a reasonable man. He must realise that I didn't know she was married. If he doesn't, I'm sure I could convince him. You're using him as an excuse because you are afraid of committing yourself.'

Self-preservation forced her to ignore his accusation. 'He was—still *is*—in love with her, damn you! How do you think he'd react if every time he thought of me—and you—all he could see was you and Susan in bed together? With calm good sense?'

'Oh, for God's sake, Clary, he must have known that things were not right with his marriage! One of the few things she said about him was that he came along at a time she needed a refuge. A man would have to be totally insensitive not to know when his wife felt like that.'

'What difference does that make to his loving her?' She turned to face him, her eyes as hard as his had ever been. 'How would you like it if I went off with—with that man we met at the Oxtens'? Tony Graham? How would you feel?'

'I'd kill him,' he said simply.

So quietly ferocious was his voice that she gaped. The implacable words sent a shiver of fear through her but she pushed on. 'And me? Would you kill me too?'

'You?' His teeth were bared in a simulacrum of a smile. 'Oh, no, I wouldn't kill you. Never. But I'd make you wish for death over and over again, Clary.'

'You're crazy,' she whispered, mesmerised by the primitive ferocity of his face. He was all barbarian, transfixed by a basic and ungovernable possessiveness. And then, as she watched, the rage was replaced by an appalled astonishment.

'No,' he muttered, extending a hand to stop her as she took a backwards step. '*No*, don't look at me like that. Oh, Clary, what you do to me! I'm sorry, darling. I'm sorry. God, all these threats . . .'

He brought her hand to his mouth and held it against his cheek as though it was a lifeline. His eyes were closed. He looked anguished. After a moment he said, 'That, I'm afraid, was the uncivilised reaction. I know that you wouldn't betray me as Susan did your brother. You have courage and honesty. And you belong to me. You knew what you were doing when you took me into yourself back there.'

The stark intensity of his words curled nerves the length of her spine. What had she awoken, with her antics under the moon?

'You shouldn't play with forces you don't fully understand,' he told her, watching from beneath lids that drooped to hide the blazing glitter in his eyes. 'Did you really think that you could unleash something as elemental as sex and not let loose all the other primitive emotions too? This is not a game, Clary.'

She jerked her hand free, whipping up anger. 'It has been until now, for you!'

'I'm glad you appreciate that this time it's different for me. And it was never a game. A pastime, perhaps, but I've always liked and respected my lovers. Don't try to change the subject, my lovely. You know that this has nothing to do with the pleasant liaisons I've enjoyed in the past. This is a compulsion, a bewitchment. We saw each other and we recognised each other, it's as simple as that. If you hadn't known it you wouldn't have reacted so violently when you saw Susan and me together, you wouldn't have allowed yourself to be blackmailed into staying here with me . . .'

She swung away again, afraid and angry, her face chalk-white beneath the moon, and began to run down the path, careless of the rocks and trees, fleeing from herself as much as him.

The hand clasping the unlit torch cracked against the rough trunk of one of the tree ferns and she drew a harsh, sobbing breath but did not stop her flight until she was out of the bush and running across the sweet grass of the paddock. Then, the haze of panic fading, she slowed down and he caught up with her in one smooth step. All that way he had been so close behind her, yet she had heard nothing.

'What did you mean, I wouldn't have stayed here? You made it impossible for me to go. You blackmailed me.'

'And did you bother to check with your brother to see whether my threats had any foundation?'

Dumbfounded, she stared up into the merciless cast of his features. He wasn't even breathing fast, she noted vaguely, and the sensation of being hunted struck her again.

'Didn't your blackmail have any basis?' Lassitude and a deep weariness flattened her voice. She allowed him to urge her across the damp grass with an arm about her shoulders because there seemed nothing else she could do.

'Yes, I'm afraid it did.' He sounded almost regretful. 'I don't make threats I can't carry out. But when you let me get away with blackmail I knew you had accepted that we belonged together. The modern woman doesn't allow herself to be blackmailed.'

'I love Angus,' she said defiantly.

He nodded, began to speak, then apparently thought better of it. After a few seconds his arm tightened across her shoulders. 'You love Angus, but you belong to me. You called yourself a virgin sacrifice—well, I've accepted your sacrifice. All that you are, all that you can be, you gave to me freely, without conditions. You can't play with myth and magic under the moon and expect to get away unscathed.' He chuckled softly. 'All enchantresses have to discover that, just as you do.'

It was nonsense, she knew that, but beneath the mockery in the deep voice was an uncompromising determination which silenced her.

The house was dark when they saw it. Clary said, 'Oh lord, I told your mother I wouldn't be long,' and tried to quicken her step.

'It's all right, you can't see her window from here. She's probably still up, it's not very late.'

It seemed as though an age had passed since she had left the house, but a glance at her watch revealed that he was correct, it was not late at all. In spite of that he locked up, and half-supported her up the stairs. She was glad of his strength; she felt waves of exhaustion wash over her.

'I'll check her,' he said softly as she looked towards his mother's door.

She let him persuade her and walked on, stopping to whisper a low good night outside her room.

He laughed beneath his breath and and caught her close to him, his mouth meeting hers in the softest of kisses.

'No,' she whispered.

'Yes.'

If he had been rough or cruel she could have borne it better, but he held her face captive between his hands and taunted her with little kisses until she swayed towards him, eyes closing. Then he enfolded her gently and pressed a chain of kisses from the cleft in her chin down the heated silk of her throat while one hand stroked the sensitive nape of her neck. By the time he lifted his head she would have followed him naked across mountains, and he knew it. Her dazzled expression gave her away as clearly as if she had spoken the words.

'Now off to bed,' he commanded roughly, as though it hurt him to speak.

She sighed and raised a languid hand to touch the place in his throat where his pulse beat. 'Are you coming?'

'No, my beautiful witch, I am not.' But he could not hide the longing in his voice as he opened her door and pushed her through it. 'Good night.'

The next morning she stretched herself awake, wincing slightly at the protests of over-used muscles.

Colour washed the smooth contours of her face and throat but she was not afflicted with the guilt she had expected. She felt marvellous, sleek and languorous and satisfied, all physical tensions resolved. A reminiscent smile curled the corners of her mouth as she stretched again with feline pleasure, examining her body for the faint bruises of passion. They were there, but surprisingly few, considering the ferocity of their union. Morgan had not been a gentle lover, but then, neither had she! He too would bear bruises, both teeth and finger marks. Afterwards, when she realised how she had marred his skin, she had searched for and kissed each small angry mark . . . She smiled again and slowly got out of bed.

Some time during the night the sky had clouded over and towards dawn rain had fallen in several heavy, sharp bursts. Now there was a mist over the garden and the valley, an ethereal Chinese vapour which shifted capriciously with the faint flurry of a wind from the north. Birds foraged for worms across the lawn, ignoring the two large cats that lay coiled together in the warmest part of the garage. The open door revealed that Morgan's car had gone. Clary turned away, fighting disappointment. He might at least have said goodbye, she thought dismally.

Over breakfast, Mrs Hargreaves told her that he wouldn't be back for several days. 'He's on the way to Tokyo,' she said. 'Didn't he tell you last night?'

'I—we talked about other things. He must have forgotten.'

It was a day of frustrations. After breakfast a telephone call, answered by Clary, turned out to be from Karen Graham. She asked for Morgan.

Not without an ignoble satisfaction Clary said cheerfully, 'I'm sorry, he's not here.'

'Oh. Who is speaking, please?'

'Clary Grey.'

A slight silence before the pleasant voice said, 'Of

course, we met at the Oxtens', didn't we. How are you? I'm afraid I have the world's worst memory. I've just realised that today is the day Morgan flies to Japan. He told me a couple of days ago that he was going but time seems to have flown by so fast!'

She finished with the graceful hope that they would meet again before Clary's job was over. And that was that. But the knowledge that Morgan had been seeing her, however innocently, made Clary raw and angry. Under her employer's direction she attacked weeds in the garden with such vigour that she broke two nails and cut the palm of her hand.

'Wear gloves,' Mrs Hargreaves said unsympathetically, 'I always do.'

'My hands don't work so well in gloves.'

'You get used to them. Do you mind driving me to the doctor's tomorrow? Ruth has to go to our local doctor so she won't be able to. I could use Morgan's driver but it seems unnecessary.'

'Of course I will. Once you've driven in Rome Auckland has no terrors.'

Mrs Hargreaves grinned. 'You're a good driver. I'm having lunch with Phil after he's checked me over, so you'll have a couple of hours to fill in. Do you want to ring your mother and arrange lunch with her?'

'She's away at Waitangi at a conference. I'll ring my brother.'

The telephone was not immediately answered; indeed, she was just about to hang up when the receiver was lifted.

'Angus?'

He sounded abstracted but he recognised her tentative voice. 'What is it, love?'

She told him of her free time and he said instantly, 'We'll have lunch together, shall we? I'll take you to—no, how would you like to go up One Tree Hill and have a picnic? There's an exceptionally good delicatessen down the road and I've been looking for an excuse to try some of their more exotic goodies.'

'That would be lovely,' she said, laughing because she found his love of picnics one of his endearing traits.

So it was arranged. The following day he picked her up in his gleaming old Jaguar from outside the specialist's impressive suite of rooms and drove her through the busy city streets until they reached the quiet, lovely open spaces of Cornwall Park with its little extinct volcano rising in grassy terraces above the houses. Angus found a sheltered spot beneath a wide jacaranda tree with a splendid view of the western reaches of Auckland, and while she spread out a rug he removed a hamper from the boot and ordered her to sit down so that he could have a look at her.

They surveyed each other, and said both together, 'You're thinner,' then laughed a little, because it had been one of their childhood tricks, this identical reaction and comment. It eased the slight awkwardness which had fretted at Clary's nerves.

'I gather from Mother that you like your Mrs Hargreaves,' he said, unpacking the hamper with deft swiftness.

'Oh, she's a darling. Very forthright and practical. My job is really a sinecure, she's no more ill than I am.'

'Then why the fine-drawn look?' he said, handing her a glazed chicken wing and a wholemeal roll.

She said nothing, stripping the meat from the bones with delicate greed before asking, 'Have you been working too hard?'

He smiled rather cynically. 'Yes.'

'How is it going?'

'Quite well,' he told her politely, piling cottage cheese and tomato on his roll. 'What's the matter, love?'

She almost told him then, but he looked so strained

that she couldn't bring herself to add to his burdens. Instead she said bluntly, 'I saw Susan in London.'

'Did you?'

She loved him, but the days when she could read his mind were long past. Strong white teeth bit into his roll; with no apparent reaction he chewed and swallowed, then asked calmly, 'And how was she?'

'She'd lost weight too.'

The irony wasn't lost on him. He even smiled a little. 'Good,' he said pleasantly. 'I hope the slut wastes away to a wraith. Then perhaps I might get some peace.'

'*Angus!*' It was hopeless, of course it was hopeless. Morgan had been wrong; where Susan was concerned Angus was not reasonable. The tiny shoot of optimism she had nurtured withered and died. 'Oh, Angus,' she said helplessly.

His wide shoulders moved in an indifferent shrug. 'What do you expect? I'm not the forgiving sort. I could perhaps be persuaded to relent if she'd fallen out of love with me and into love with bloody Caird, but clearly she only saw me as a convenient way station on her road to wealth. So, if it comes to that, was he, but he had the sense not to fall in love with her.'

In spite of the warmth of the sun Clary shivered. 'You sound so bitter,' she said stupidly.

He lifted eyes as darkly shadowed as her own, blue as the icy depths of the polar sea. 'It's either bitterness or Dad's way of coping with the same situation. I prefer bitterness. Don't ever fall in love, Clary, it's not worth the pain.'

'Does it have to be like that?'

'For me it does.' He finished the rest of his roll while she ate a cherry tomato, then asked, 'Who was she sleeping with when you saw her?'

'I don't think—she was in a little flat——'

'So he dumped her.' He laughed sardonically.

'She's going to some college to learn how to be a

beauty therapist.' Pleadingly Clary put her hand on his wrist, wishing quite desperately that she had never mentioned Susan. 'Angus, she said that she was sorry, and I really believe that she is. Do you have to hate her?'

His hand turned and gripped hers so ferociously that she had to bite her lip to keep from crying out. 'At the moment,' he said strangely, 'I do have to.'

She was silent at the bleak misery in his face. He needed the stimulus of his hatred to feed on. And that hatred was extended to Morgan. It was not rational, but love corroded by betrayal and jealousy is never rational.

'I'm sorry,' she said softly.

'Have I frightened you?' He leaned over and kissed her cheek, releasing her maltreated hand to give her shoulders a quick squeeze. 'Sorry, love, but I can't be sensible and sophisticated about either of them. She's a bitch and he's a swine and the only thing which keeps me going is my intention to one day prove to both of them that I am not the weak cuckold they believe me to be.'

CHAPTER NINE

THEY ate the rest of the picnic in near silence, letting the peace and the silence soak into the tension between them. After a while Angus began to tell her of his new invention and the plans his backers were making for its marketing.

'Could you have done it by yourself?' Clary asked casually. 'Without their backing?'

He shrugged. 'Perhaps, but it would have been a lot more difficult.'

When he saw that she was interested he described the processes needed to get even such potentially life-saving equipment as this on to the market as quickly and cheaply as possible.

'I'm no businessman,' he said, 'but I'm learning. These people have contacts all over the world, access to information and money I would have had to struggle for. They've saved me an immense amount of effort and time. And that's valuable, because the sooner this piece of equipment is used the sooner it's going to start saving lives. Every major airline in the world wants it!'

'My brother the genius,' Clary murmured, hiding her deep unease with a teasing inflection.

He grinned. 'Hardly. I'm very much a novice in the business world, but it's been fascinating to see how business gears up for something like this.'

'Any ideas about the next invention?'

'Lasers,' he said briskly, and delivered a lecture on their uses and prospects which fascinated her even though she understood very little of it.

'I see,' she said untruthfully when he finally ran down.

His smile was tinged with affectionate mockery. 'I don't suppose you do, but you're an excellent listener. Come on, finish that coffee or we'll keep your dragon waiting.'

'She is not a dragon. I like her enormously.'

'She sounds like a dragon. And someone is draining the colour from your face.' He packed the remnants of their lunch, putting the hamper back in the car while she folded the rug.

'I enjoyed that,' he said as they left the park. 'You are the most restful woman I know. We must do it again. When does this job finish?'

'Can you step on things a bit? We're late,' Clary said, adding, 'I promised to stay for three months.'

'And then?'

'Back to nursing, I suppose. I'm thinking about it.'

He realised that she didn't want to discuss her future, and so they chatted about inconsequential things all the way back to the specialist's rooms.

'Pull into the car park at the side of the building,' she directed when they were a few hundred yards from the rooms. 'Our car's there.'

So was the specialist's, a famous name who drove an equally famous vintage Rolls out of which he was helping Mrs Hargreaves.

'There she is,' Clary said cheerfully, giving her brother a swift kiss on the cheek. 'Goodbye, take care.'

He didn't reply, or more probably she hurtled out of the car so quickly that she didn't catch his answer, but after a moment she heard his car begin to turn out of the car park. She waved and smiled over her shoulder as she walked rapidly towards her employer.

Back at Hunter's Valley she recalled Angus's hard profile as he drove away; so bleak, so lonely. She could have wept for him.

And herself. That night, desolation murdered sleep; for hours she lay in her dark, beautiful room, staring with aching eyes at the ceiling as she forced herself to accept that she could not marry Morgan. She could not take her happiness at the cost of her brother's. He would see her love for Morgan as a betrayal equivalent to Susan's treachery, and he was in no mood to be rational about anything to do with Morgan. He had really frightened her with his ferocious desire for revenge, almost manic in its intensity.

What if he discovered that Morgan was behind the so-called consortium? No, there was little chance of that. Morgan must have buried his involvement very deep because Angus was no fool, if there had been any trace of Morgan he would have found it.

Wearily the thoughts chased themselves around her brain. Angus was fighting because, as Morgan had pointed out, he was not passive, he was a battler, but her loving eyes had seen beneath the aggression to his pain and she could not bring herself to do anything which might add to it. Perhaps, when his anger had faded . . .

But that might take years. And would Morgan wait that long? She still did not know whether he really wanted to marry her, or whether he saw it as a symbol of surrender. Perhaps he resented her affection for Angus. It was not impossible, although she had seen no signs of the sort of twisted possessiveness which that implied. He seemed unable to appreciate the depths of feeling he had roused in Angus; possibly because he had never loved as intensely as the younger man.

No, she thought, remembering, that was not so. His was no pallid desire. But he was not romantic, as Angus must be. She could not imagine Morgan suffering so bitterly if she left him, except in his pride. That, of course, was where he thought Angus had been hurt. Clary had not considered this before. Now, during the long night, she examined the idea with a gradual wonder, only to feel that she was hampered by the fact that she had never been in love before, so she could not recognise love in others.

You are in love now. How did she know? How did she know that what she felt was more than the lust she had wanted it to be? As she lay awake in the four-poster bed and the stars turned in their courses in the dark sky, she probed the depths of her emotions, teasing out the strands of affection and desire, tenderness and fear, respect, interest—the multitudinous threads which weave together to form love. Towards dawn she discovered that if marriage to Morgan would harm him, she would not do it. She wanted him to be happy. It was as simple as that. And it *was* love.

But when she tried to apply her new understanding to her brother she suffered from an even greater handicap. Except on that fleeting visit to London on their honeymoon she had never seen Susan and Angus together; she had no idea of the dynamics of their marriage. She knew only that Susan had entered into it for the wrong reasons and left Angus because she had been smothered and frustrated. Clary could not approve of the method she had chosen to put an end to it, but slowly she was forced to accept that her sister-in-law had the right to search for a more satisfying life. And that Angus's reaction bore all the hallmarks of outraged and possessive masculinity, thwarted and furious. Not of love.

But having accepted that, there was still nothing she could do about it. Angus thought he had loved Susan, so he was suffering just as much as if he had. And he would bleed if his sister married the man who had lured Susan away from him.

The day stretched before her, empty. She felt desperate, as though she had to reach some decision before Morgan came back from Japan. She thought she knew him well enough now to be able to ignore any threats of blackmail; he had almost admitted that such tactics had been a serious mistake, born of desperation.

All day, as she weeded, helped Ruth clean silver and learned the intricacies of making cape-gooseberry jam, she wondered whether there was any way out of the situation which did not involve a wait of years until Angus had had a chance to get over his disillusionment. She frowned as she picked dead blooms from the yesterday-today-and-tomorrow bush, her eyes drifting unseeingly over the white and lilac and purple flowers, and was still frowning when she emerged exhausted from the pool after swimming endless laps in an effort to get rid of her frustration. She had never felt so impotent in her life, and it galled her and frightened her.

After dinner she played three games of patience on the exquisite little loo-table in the drawing-room, winning all of them, then, gazing pensively at the muted shades of dusk, went out through the french windows into the garden.

Ruth's voice summoned her back. 'Telephone,' it said succinctly.

It was Morgan; so clear was his voice that at first she thought he had come back.

'Where are you?' she asked stupidly.

'In a hotel room in Tokyo. Missing you.'

'Oh.' After a moment's pause she said, 'Your mother is well. I took her to——'

'I've already spoken to her. I want to know how you are. Not pining for me, by any chance?'

'Of course not,' she said too quickly, and had to endure his low, satisfied chuckle.

'I like it when you try to slap me down to size. It tells me I'm too close to that prickly heart of yours. What have you been doing today?'

She told him and he asked, 'Do you like gardening? Don't let that bulldozer of a mother——'

'I've always liked gardening. My mother is an expert.'

'Good. She and mine will have lots in common.

Does yours want to be buried under a tree of her own choosing too?'

Clary choked her crow of laughter but he heard it and chuckled, before asking, 'So you aren't bored? Normally, of course, there's far more happening around the homestead than at present.'

'I know, Ruth's told me. Quite a few of your mother's friends have called in to see her. They don't stay long, but they entertain her.' She described one elegant and haughty dowager, realising only when she had finished that he might not appreciate acerbic comments about his mother's friends, however amusing.

His amused voice reassured her. 'Marvellous, isn't she? Her husband is the bane of her life, a diamond deliberately and defiantly in the rough. They fight like cat and dog and thoroughly enjoy it. You'll like him when you meet him, and you will be meeting him. You'll be meeting all our friends. How was Angus?'

'How—oh, your mother, I suppose.' She frowned at the realisation that Mrs Hargreaves had told him about Angus, but continued tonelessly, 'He seems well. I'd say he's lost a stone he needs, but he appears to be coping.'

'I find it rather reassuring that such an aloof creature as you should be so devoted a sister. Is it because it's a nice, safe relationship?'

'I love my mother too.'

The frosty words didn't impress him. 'Another safe bond, easily managed. So Angus is coping. Good.'

'He's very bitter.'

'Bitterness provides a convenient prop when things go wrong. He'll grow out of it.'

She bit her lip. 'I hope so. I'm afraid you underrate his capacity for emotion. It doesn't seem to me that it's a prop, it's more like an incentive. He wants to prove . . .' Her voice trailed into silence as she realised her disloyalty.

He picked up her meaning, of course. 'Does he, indeed?' he said thoughtfully. 'My poor little love, I think something will have be done about Angus.'

'*No!*'

Tension sizzled through the short silence that followed until he said in measured tones, 'I'm not actually into the business of bumping people off, Clary. Or forcing them into bankruptcy, if that's what you were thinking in that rather commonplace mind of yours. You've been too long overseas. In New Zealand we don't do things that way.'

'No. Blackmail, of course, is perfectly permissible.'

There was another ominous silence before he said lightly, 'You don't intimidate easily, do you? I'm sorry.'

'So am I. I over-reacted.'

She could hear his smile in his voice, and knew exactly how it would crease his lean cheeks, could see the gleam of mockery in his narrowed eyes. 'The story of our relationship. Never mind, I've become inured to the way you automatically assume the worst about me. Such as that I'm prepared to bump your brother off. I can only hope that closer acquaintanceship disabuses you of such misconceptions.'

He was being deliberately provocative, the formal polysyllables distancing her, but beneath the amused sarcasm she heard anger and hurt.' She didn't want him to hang up thinking that she believed him capable of the sort of ruthless behaviour her impetuous denial had indicated.

'Morgan?' she said tentatively.

'Clary?'

'I'm sorry. I didn't really believe—I know you wouldn't do anything to Angus.'

Another little silence before he drawled, 'I have every intention of doing something to Angus, my lovely. I consider him a damned nuisance. I can't even promise that it won't cause him some pain. However, I intend to use the universal excuse, that it will be for his own good. More to the point, it will be for *my* good. Most importantly, it will be for your good. I've had enough of seeing you torn two ways. Promise you won't leave before I come back.'

She hesitated, her finger lightly touching the dial on the telephone, picking out the numbers which would connect her to her mother. Then she said, 'No, I won't leave.'

The trouble was that she knew his capacity for ruthlessness. Everything about him proclaimed a hard relentless authority. A man who could swashbuckle his way through the financial jungle to build himself an empire needed to be tough as well as clever; it had been no weakling who had used blackmail to keep her with him. He had not liked it, he regretted it, but he had not flinched from using it.

Yet he had made no attempt to blackmail her into his bed. He had waited until she was ready. He could be kind, and shatteringly gentle, and his matter-of-fact attitude towards his mother failed entirely to hide his deep love for her.

After she had hung up Clary traced the outline of a fine Parian-ware Venus on the console table in the hall. It was humiliating to have to admit how much she missed him. That little smile she had never seen on herself curved the corners of her mouth. A Venus smile, the smile of a woman who knows how to seduce. When he came back she would show him how much she missed him—how much she ached for him.

The roar of a car being driven far too fast up the drive brought her head up, changing her expression to one of alarm when she recognised the note of the engine. An icy sensation expanded in her stomach, was reflected in the sudden pallor of her face as she ran to the door.

Angus was already halfway across the courtyard, his lean body moving with dangerous purpose. Her eyes suddenly swallowing her face, Clary stopped abruptly, then forced herself on.

'What is it?' she demanded, running down the steps. 'Mum? Has something happened to Mum?'

He grabbed the hand that was shaking his arm and pivoted around, dragging her across to the car. 'No, she's fine,' he snarled, almost pushing her into the passenger's seat.

As he strode around to his side she realised that somehow he had discovered everything. Nervously she protested, 'Angus, I'll have to let someone know that I'm going.'

'Who? Morgan Caird?'

She waited while he put the car into gear, biting her lips at the scream of maltreated tyres. When they were almost to the end of the drive she said, 'No, he's overseas just now.'

'A pity. It means I can't smash his face in this time.'

She risked a quick look at him, her heart quailing at the implacable cast of his features.

'Where are we going?' she asked almost inaudibly.

'Off his land.'

She said nothing more until she could tell him that they were past the boundary. He appeared to take no notice but at the next suitable spot he pulled off the road and cut the engine, staring through the windscreen at the rapidly darkening countryside ahead of them.

Clary remained silent until he asked silkily, 'Now tell me why you are living with him, Clary.'

'Because his mother, Mrs Hargreaves, is recovering from a heart attack.'

'That's the woman Jim Patten mentioned? The one I told you about.'

'The same one.' Her voice was very steady but she had to deliberately relax her fingers to prevent any tell-tale tension from showing.

He still refused to look at her but she sensed a slight relaxation in his taut frame. 'I see. And why, when you realised who she was, didn't you leave?'

'Because I promised her I would stay.'

'Because you were sleeping with her son.'

'No.' Her instinct was to cry her innocence to the stars, but she dared not admit emotion to the subject. She knew this dangerous quietness; it meant that he was barely in control. Very clearly she said, 'She is my patient, Angus. If I had known who she was I would not have taken the position, but I didn't know, and once I'd agreed I couldn't back out just because she's Morgan Caird's mother.'

It sounded reasonable. As he cursed Morgan with monotonous fluency she sat tensely, waiting.

'Are you sleeping with him?'

'No.'

The word fell into the frightening silence, clear, cold, tinged with impatience. A lie, yet not entirely untruthful, because there would be no more lovemaking.

'When I realised where you were I felt as though you had betrayed me. I couldn't bear it. I should have known better.'

His voice trembled. She said wretchedly, 'Oh— Angus!' and leaned towards him. For a moment he resisted, then bent his head so that the hot tears scorched into her shoulder.

She ran her fingers through the bronze hair so like her own in colour and texture, whispered soft endearments and comforted him as best she could while the light faded from her world.

At last he muttered, 'Sorry,' and moved away, embarrassed and wary. 'God, I hate him,' he said thickly. 'Did you know he's provided the money to back me?'

For a moment she wanted to lie but she did not trust her voice to do it again. So she nodded.

'Taunted you with it, did he? Well, there's no way I can get out of it, but I'll make the swine pay——'

'How?' When he didn't answer she said urgently, 'Angus, how? You mustn't do anything stupid.'

He turned his head and gave her a travesty of a smile, so cynical she could have wept. 'Don't worry, I know that nothing would give him greater pleasure than to get rid of me. I'm not so stupid as to give him the opportunity. He's a clever bastard and he's got me this time. He must have laughed like a hyena when the fish took the bait he dangled so temptingly.' One big fist hit the wheel. 'Well, he's had his fun with me. I'll take all the help he can give me and when I've enough power I'll cut free and he can go whistle for some other poor fish to cuckold.'

His agony hurt Clary profoundly, but although she shivered at such unbalanced, naked hatred she didn't dare try to present a more reasonable appreciation of Morgan. Angus needed his hatred to blanket the anguish of losing Susan. When that eased, as such pain always does, then surely his hatred would fade too.

'I'm sorry I came on so heavy,' he said after a while. 'I must have scared the hell out of you.'

'You did, rather,' she admitted. 'Now you know why I didn't feel I could tell you.'

'When I saw his mother yesterday I nearly passed out. I recognised her from a newspaper photograph— I'd forgotten she had married again. Then I remembered it was Jim Patten who had mentioned that she needed a nurse, and I did a bit of delving.' Suggestively his hand flexed, forming a clenched fist. 'He didn't want to tell me but I persuaded him in the end.'

Clary's blood ran cold. 'How?' she breathed.

'Oh, don't worry, I didn't hurt him. After I'd pointed out that I couldn't pull out now even if Caird was up to his elbows in it, he told me. He's not into heroics.'

'When was this?'

'A couple of hours ago.' He looked across to where she sat huddled into her seat, white-faced and cold. 'I thought he'd won again, that not content with stealing my wife he'd taken my sister. What do you think of him?'

The raw jealousy in his voice made her wince. She didn't dare take time for thought. 'He's very attractive,' she said remotely. 'Hard. Ruthless. What do you want me to say?'

'That you hate him, I suppose.'

'That's not true.'

If he suspected anything he chose not to pursue it, contenting himself with a long, difficult scrutiny. At last, when she thought she might break down and tell him the truth, he said quietly, 'I'm sorry, I have no right to expect you to join in my battles. I'll take you back.'

'A good idea. You look as if you could do with some coffee . . .'

'I don't feel like setting foot inside his boundaries, let alone accepting the smallest amount of hospitality,' he said in that expressionless voice she had never heard him use before.

Nobody had missed her, or if they had noticed her abrupt departure they hadn't been bothered by it. Ruth was with Mrs Hargreaves in her bedroom; as Clary walked listlessly through the garden she could hear the soft sound of their voices on the cool, sweetly-smelling air. Busy with plans for the new house, no doubt. They were both having a high old time.

The monument to Mrs Hargreaves' perfectionist attitudes was all about Clary as she wandered across lawns wet with dew, past borders bright with summer flowers, beneath trees chosen for their grace and form. The villa by the sea would be as perfect in its way as this, but it was unlikely that she would ever see it.

Surely the saddest sound in the world is the

croaking of frogs! In the lily pond a chorus of them
sang a mournful little bracket and the tears came,
bitter as wormwood. She collapsed on to a seat
beneath a weeping willow and sobbed into her hands
as if she had lost the only thing that had ever mattered
to her.

It was stupid to grieve because she had wanted a
romantic dream and it had been smirched. Real life
bore no resemblance to fairy tales. It never had. That
was why romance was so popular; it gave the greys of
everyday life a colouring of glamour.

Late though it was when she came in, Ruth was still
up. She gave Clary a rather too intent glance and said,
'Did you have bad news? Your brother . . .? That was
him in the car, wasn't it? Mrs Hargreaves said . . .'

'Yes, it was him. And no, there was no bad news. I
suppose I'm homesick.'

'Ah well, it hits us all. Hop up into bed and I'll
bring you a cup of tea.'

'That's sweet of you, but don't bother, I don't really
need it.'

'You look as though you need something stronger
than tea,' Ruth said gently as she went towards the
kitchen.

Mrs Hargreaves did not mention Clary's state,
although she must have noticed. After she had
showered and gone through her usual beauty routine,
Clary came back into her room to find a tray with a
small pot of tea waiting for her.

Her nose wrinkled at the pleasant scent. Camomile
tea, just the thing to encourage sleep. Ruth must have
been quite concerned about her! No wonder. Her
mirror had revealed a drawn, tired face, still faintly
pink about the eyelids and nose, the tiny lines at the
corners of her eyes accented.

By morning they had faded into their normal
obscurity, but during the next few days Clary learned
several things about herself. One was that it was

possible to appear quite normal when desolation seemed an actual physical weight in her chest. The other was that it helped to be as cheerful and as pleasant as she could; it took the edge off the pain and lessened a tendency to self-pity.

The hardest thing to cope with was her infinite capacity for recollection. Now that she had made the decision to turn away from what Morgan offered her, she was tormented by a hunger so intense it was like starvation. With it came total sensory recall, so that in those timeless moments between sleep and awareness when the conscious mind relaxes she relived her seduction over and over again, her feverish senses stimulated anew by the memory of his ardour and her surrender, the heated, eerie atmosphere, his mastery of her senses as he had taken her with him into that unexplored realm of passion.

When she closed her eyes she saw his face as it had been during that long initiation, by turns tender and hungry and fierce, culminating in the taut, agonised rictus of ecstasy when his body had shuddered into hers.

Night after night she twisted restlessly in her chaste bed, afire with the memory of the exquisite sensations his hands had created, the way he had used his mouth to force her into a dimension of sensuality she had never imagined, and the final pulsing rapture which had torn an unrestrained cry from her throat.

That was bad enough. What was worse were the dreams, some filled with that same voluptuous sensuality so that she woke trembling, sobbing with frustration. And the others, when she watched helplessly as his long powerful body lay against Susan, against Karen, entwined with women whose faces were mistily obscure but always enraptured.

They were the worst. Deep in her personality an intense possessiveness was outraged by his behaviour before he had known her. A wildness in her responded to and matched his unshackled masculinity; what her conscious mind found difficult to accept, her subconscious admitted freely. They were two of a kind and he had sullied that spiritual communion by his careless misuse of his sexuality.

Common sense told her that she was wrong. He had played a game with clearly defined rules, intending no hurt. What had happened before she met him was no concern of hers. She did not even have to ask herself if he had touched another woman since he had met her; she knew that he had not. It was beyond foolishness to expect a virile man in his thirties to be inexperienced, especially a man like Morgan, whose authority and incandescent sexuality was so attractive to women.

Yet she felt betrayed. She had waited, why had not he?

'You don't look as though you're sleeping at all well,' Mrs Hargreaves observed over breakfast one morning, adding without pause, 'we're going into town. Pack a nightdress and something pretty to wear out to dinner.'

After the peace of the homestead Auckland was noisy and brash and wearying. Morgan's apartment was in an exclusive tower block built hard by one of the little green volcanoes which dotted Auckland's isthmus.

'Ten minutes from town yet quiet,' Mrs Hargreaves said with satisfaction. 'How do you like it?'

It couldn't have been a greater contrast to the homestead. That had the comfortable ambience of antiques and another age; the apartment breathed an opulent modern discretion, with superb Italian furniture, a sophisticated interplay of fabrics and surfaces in dark blue and bronze backed by pale, cool suede wall hangings which reminded Clary of the thick petals of a magnolia flower.

'Did you do this?' she asked, not attempting to hide her pleasure.

Mrs Hargreaves chuckled. 'No, this is Morgan's. He had it redecorated when he got back from the United Kingdom last year. He had a good decorator to do it, but she did more or less as she was told.'

'It's beautiful.'

'I'm glad you think so. I assume it was designed to set you off. Your hair is the exact colour of that bronze over there. Can't see myself what he sees in it, I don't appreciate work that's not representational, but it certainly suits the room. And the blue is the colour of your eyes. He's like me, he can carry a colour in his head. It's quite a rare knack. Now, unless you want to wear jeans out to the airport, you'd better change.'

'The airport?'

'Yes, didn't I tell you that Morgan is coming back today?' She smiled rather wickedly. 'I should, I suppose, let you go out to meet him by yourself, but I enjoy airports. And if I know Morgan, there'll be a small deputation there to meet him. Or with him. We've got ten minutes to get ready before his driver comes to pick us up.'

Clary changed into the blue shirt-waister she had worn to the Oxtens' place, slipped on shoes and renewed her lipstick. She felt rather numb; sleepless nights and unhappiness had the effect of barricading her off from the normal emotions. For a long moment she looked into the mirror at her reflection, then, with a sensation of walls closing around her, went fatalistically out.

As always the airport was busy, but Clary took no pleasure in her favourite sport of people-watching. It was ridiculous, but she was terrified that the big jet from Tokyo would crash on landing. From the windows in the lounge they were led to where there was a good view of one of the runways; she sat ignoring it, her eyes seeing nothing.

Even there the fruitless spiral of her thoughts tormented her. Angus was too precious to her, his mental health too precarious to jeopardise. It might be years before he recovered enough to accept Morgan as a brother-in-law. She did not dare become Morgan's mistress because in his arms she became witless. Once he realised that he wouldn't hesitate to persuade her into marriage.

But oh, his hunger excited her, and her heart sang and light flared in the depths of her eyes.

'Here he is,' his mother said tersely.

He came in through the door, tall, vital, commanding. Clary's backbone seemed to melt.

'Mother,' he said, and kissed her before turning to where Clary was trying to efface herself behind a couple of eager executive types who waited for him.

'Darling,' he said deeply, and as if he couldn't help himself his hand curved around the nape of her neck and his mouth bruised hers in a hard, stinging kiss which hurt even as it pleasured her.

Branding her, she thought vaguely, opening her eyes.

'Been good?' he asked softly, his smile tinged with a blend of mockery and desire, eyes blazing green in the dark lineaments of his face.

Clary became aware of a paralysed silence about them. 'Have you?' she retorted crisply, pulling away, but there was a throbbing note in her voice which had never been there before and mockery changed to triumph as he released her.

After that his entourage treated her with a stunned respect which told her that no other woman had been greeted in that way before them. She shivered, feeling the walls close even more narrowly around her.

CHAPTER TEN

THE entourage travelled back to the city in another car, no doubt speculating all the way, except for one man who had impaled Clary with one sharp, not unkindly glance and then avoided looking her way. He sat in front beside the driver, but spoke over his shoulder to give Morgan a swift rundown on events within his organisation.

In the middle of the back seat Clary tried to hold herself away from too close a contact with Morgan. He knew what she was doing, of course, but beyond a taunting smile seemed content to allow her this small freedom.

I must be mad, she thought as his personal assistant's voice droned on, when even the touch of his arm against my shoulder drives me insane with desire.

It wasn't having the same effect on him. She dared not look into his face but he seemed totally relaxed. One hand lay on his thigh, the long fingers loose, as he made crisp pertinent comments, his brain outpacing the older man's. Clary found herself listening closely. This was a new Morgan, and she was greedy, she wanted to understand all aspects of his complex personality. Frowning slightly she concentrated, appreciating for the first time just how penetrating and subtle that acute intelligence was.

He and his assistant spoke a kind of verbal shorthand which at first confused her, but after some minutes of close attention she comprehended enough to be impressed and a little awed.

Deep down she admitted to another emotion. It was shameful, but she basked in the knowledge that she could suspend the operation of that formidable intellect, overturn that force of will with nothing more than the promise of her femininity.

Barbaric, she thought, trying to whip up contempt for herself. If her power was great, so was her responsibility to use it wisely. And if she did not then she was no better than the temptresses of old, the Messalinas and Loreleis who had used their sexuality to lure men to their doom. There was certainly something pagan and dangerous about her emotions; that, she thought wearily, was why she was so afraid of them.

Her gaze kindled with blue fire as she lifted it to the beautiful severity of his profile. He turned his head with a sharp little movement so that their eyes met. At the naked possession she saw in his glance Clary's breath caught in her throat.

Dimly she heard the voice of his personal assistant; Morgan answered and all she could think of was the sensuous movement of his lips, the contrast of his strong teeth against his skin.

Her own skin tightened and chilled, then heated into fire as he took her hand. She was aware of a slight faltering in the older man's speech, but Morgan turned his head to answer him, deep voice crisp and controlled, and Clary wondered if she had imagined the tremor which seemed to run from him to her when their hands first touched.

He didn't break the sweet contact until they arrived in the basement car park of a large central city building.

Then he said, 'I'll be home by seven,' and was gone, followed by his entourage, some of whom were a little less than subtle in their efforts to see who was in the car.

Clary said just above audibility, 'He looks like a shepherd, sweeping them off with him.'

'In a way I suppose he is. They're all very competent men, but he's the one who holds them together. Now, let's have a little saunter through the shops.'

Mrs Hargreaves's idea of a little saunter embraced a careful search of several rather grand antique shops where she displayed the kind of knowledge which impressed their proprietors, and a critical and often uncomplimentary perusal of almost the entire stock of an extremely expensive decorator's premises.

'For seating,' she explained, after introducing Clary to the decorator. 'Antique chairs and sofas were not built for comfort. Use them as ornaments if you like them, but sit on modern stuff.'

The afternoon was an education, but Clary was glad when they arrived back at the apartment. It was weak, but she wanted to be as close to Morgan as she could be in the time they had left.

He was not there. Clary showered and pulled on the dress she had brought, the coppery one she had worn at Chase, and went out into the large sitting-room and he was waiting, seated in a large chair reading the paper. He remembered the dress. As he rose to his feet he gave her a comprehensive look, his sardonic glance lingering on her taut face.

'Making a point?' he murmured. 'I'd begun to think my memories were too highly coloured to be accurate. It's a relief to find they're not.'

She smiled, because it was all she could do to hide how the sight of him affected her. The crisp black and white of his dinner jacket and shirt threw into prominence the sculptured strength of his features. His half-closed eyes flamed with triumph and desire.

Roughly she asked, 'Where are we going tonight?'

'To a very quiet dinner with an old admirer of Mama's.'

She relaxed. While she dressed she had worried about the dangers of too public a dinner. Gossip in Auckland tended to travel as fast as radio waves, and she was still afraid for Angus.

'Ashamed to be seen with me, Clary?'

The question was softly delivered but she read the danger and blinked, wilfully misunderstanding him. 'No, you look very elegant, very sexy. As I'm sure you know.'

'You think I'm a conceited ape.'

She shook her head and turned away from the gold-green gaze. 'I think you're an extremely intelligent person. You know that I——' her tongue seemed to thicken in her mouth, '—that you are very attractive,' she finished with plodding care.

'But you are strong enough to resist that animal magnetism.'

The exquisite sarcasm made her flinch. Her eyelids closed for a second over her burning eyes but when she turned back to face him she was gravely composed. 'I suppose you're entitled to a little satisfaction. If you like to hear me admit it, then no, I'm not strong enough to resist it. You know how I feel about you.'

'There is,' he said savagely, 'something peculiarly degrading about being seen as a stud.'

'You should be used to it.' The words came bitterly across her tongue.

White-faced, they stared at each other until a slight sound at the door broke into their attention. As his mother came in Morgan complimented her with a teasing urbanity which was as far removed from the naked aggression of a moment before as anything could have been.

Mrs Hargreaves appeared to notice nothing, although the tension could almost be seen. However, Clary was granted a few moments to compose herself, moments during which she realised that a confrontation had been postponed, not cancelled.

Sure enough, when, after a pleasant evening, Mrs Hargreaves left them together in the sitting-room Morgan said quietly, 'Would you mind staying a moment, Clary?'

He waited until the door closed behind his mother before suggesting, 'Why don't you sit down? And try not to look as though you are a Sabine woman after her Roman abductor reached home with her.'

She headed for a chair but he took her hand and guided her towards a sofa; once there he pulled her across his lap so that her head rested on his upper arm. Clary didn't try to resist. Even as her body fired into life she recognised the purposefulness in him.

'And so,' he said gently, his breath warm on her forehead, 'tell me why you have been so charming and polite and bloody aloof all evening.'

'Angus came to see me,' she said tonelessly.

He exhaled sharply. 'Ah. And told you . . .?'

'He knows everything.'

'Does he know that we are lovers?'

She hesitated, then shook her head. A lean finger lifted her chin. She knew how his business rivals must feel when transfixed by that piercing crystalline gaze. Clary said nothing, her misery plain. When he looked at her like that she saw beyond the forceful, sophisticated man of the world to a Morgan no one else suspected. There was triumph in his gaze, and a savage determination and beneath it the steady flame of desire, banked now, held under rigorous control. She could free it from the restraints set upon it by his will and he knew it, the knowledge was there in his face.

But it was not enough. However powerful, however ecstatic, no life could be built on sex alone. And he knew that too.

'So what happens now?' he asked.

She lifted her hand and held it against his chest, absorbing the heavy thudding of his heart through the palm. 'I'll stay with your mother until the doctor tells me I can go.'

Beneath her hand his heart seemed to stop, then began again with increased speed.

'What of us?' he demanded tightly.

She looked up into a face drawn with a terrible tension. 'There is no us,' she said sadly. 'You can take me to bed any time you like—you know it, I know it—but when it's time, I'll go and we'll never see each other again.'

The tawny fire of his head bent, was lowered until his face rested against her breasts. Clary smoothed the crisp hair with tender fingers, cradled the fine shape of his skull in her hands, listened to his harsh breathing and knew that she was on the brink of the obsession she feared. She had to go, while there was still time for her to escape.

When he lifted his head her hands slid over the sharply defined bones of his cheeks to lie along his jaw. Incredibly, he was smiling, although there was no amusement in the angular face.

'Have you ever heard of the Furies?' he asked, and at her surprised nod elaborated, 'They were Greek and there were three of them. Thoroughly unpleasant people. The Avenger of Blood, the Jealous one and the Implacable. They were very enthusiastic when it came to punishing people for neglecting claims of kinship. I think you must be a personification of them.'

The observation pierced the armour of her control. Wincing, her heart in her eyes, she lifted her head from his shoulder and kissed his beautiful mouth with a swift, unendurable passion.

'Angus hates you beyond reasoning. I told you that we were an obsessive family,' she said harshly as she tried to free herself from him.

'You are terrified of giving in to what you see as an obsession,' he accused. 'You may not realise it, but Angus is only an excuse. You saw your father die and you are afraid that if you admit that you love me the same thing will happen to you.'

'I've already told you that I love you.'

'It's a pathetic sort of love that puts a brother before a lover.'

His anger was palpable, an icy emanation rapidly demolished by an even stronger desire. Before she could do more than shift her balance his arms tightened and his mouth took hers in a compulsive, violent kiss. Instantly she was aroused; the inherent savagery she had incited did not slacken even though after the first few seconds she made no attempt to resist.

Completely fled now were the façades of courtesy and consideration. In that silent, consuming world of the senses they were as irrelevant as rational thought. Clary lifted her throat as a sacrifice, shuddering when his teeth bit just beyond gentleness down the fine pale length of it. Her fingers curved around his cheek, every tiny nerve end rejoicing at the rasp of his beard. The neckline of her dress proved no barrier as his hand slid beneath to cover her breast. At the fierce probe of his fingers she drew a ragged breath, dimly realising in the last part of her brain that was functioning that his other hand had released the zip at the back.

In a moment she was naked above the waist except for her bra, and that was soon jerked from her, freeing her breasts. Yet he did not look at them; his bright hostile gaze was riveted to her face even when his palm slid slowly across the smooth curves.

Clary's breath caught in her throat. A tide of uncontrollable pleasure surged through her. Weightless, boneless, under the experienced manipulation of his fingers her body arched, twisting convulsively in her effort to get closer to him. Her fingers moved swiftly and in a moment his shirt was open and she was pressing open-mouthed kisses to his smooth tanned shoulder, the first shudders of delight beginning to build deep inside her.

He was trembling too, his skin hot and damp

beneath her mouth; he muttered something and that tormenting hand slid from her breast down beneath the loosened material of her dress to come to rest between her thighs.

Gasping, incoherent, Clary lifted her hips against his hand, striving to assuage some of the tormenting ache, and he groaned, and pulled his hand free and dragged the dress up to cover her breasts before clamping his arms around her.

For long moments her cheek was pressed against his chest. Deafened by the racing beat of his heart she lay quiescent while the arousal peaked before slowly subsiding into dormancy, the kind of dormancy which needed only a touch to waken. He smelt faintly of sandalwood, more of sweat and the indefinable scent of masculinity.

'It's not enough,' he said at last in impeded tones.

Lips still turned against his skin she whispered, 'I'm sorry, Morgan.'

'Sorry? My God, so am I.'

That was all, but when he left her at the door of her bedroom with a curt good night he was no longer a man ridden by an obsession. He looked indomitable, she thought warily, and the smile he gave her before closing her door on her was a masterpiece of irony.

She slept late, so late that it was almost midday when she woke. After a horrified glance at her watch she leapt out of bed and hurtled into the bathroom before dressing in such a blur of activity that she was in the sitting-room before she had time to remember the scene last night.

She was brought up just inside the doorway by the sight of Morgan, alone.

Clary came to a precipitate halt, eyeing him warily as he lifted his gaze from the newspaper and directed a hooded glance her way. 'Where's your mother?' she asked breathlessly.

'Back at the valley.' He stood up, viewing her

dawning alarm with a grim smile. 'She no longer needs you.'

'She never really has.' Clary made a brave attempt to sound accusing but her eyes dropped away from his and the words were uttered far from forcefully.

'As it happened, no, but it was reassuring to have you around. Come and have some breakfast instead of hovering by the door like a frightened dog.'

'Breakfast?'

He grinned, but beneath his lashes his eyes were watchful. 'Brunch, then.'

A very elegant brunch. Coffee and croissants, a superb fantasy of fruits, strawberries, island papaya, the scented golden rectangles of its cousin the babaco, segments of tangelo, that sweetest of the citrus family.

'Such different fruits,' Clary said, tasting the babaco for the first time. 'Where did it come from?'

'Ecuador.' He began to speak of the boom in horticulture in New Zealand, the rapidly expanding number of sub-tropical fruits which were being brought into the country by dedicated plant hunters. Slowly Clary relaxed, listening as the deep sure voice charted the progress made in the horticultural industry while she had been away.

'You sound as though it's an interest of yours,' she said.

'I believe in our future as an exporter of food as well as technology. New Zealanders seem to have a talent for improvisation which can amount to genius, as in your brother. All we need is development and marketing expertise, and that I can supply.'

The sound of the doorbell made her jump. She looked an enquiry at him, unable to see beneath the smooth mask of his features.

'Ah,' he said calmly, 'bring your coffee into the sitting-room.'

An unthinking fatalism kept her quiet, although she realised that he was geared for some kind of confrontation. Beneath their heavy lids his eyes gleamed with the light of battle; she could feel his alert vitality reach out to encompass her. He looked like a swordsman about to fight a duel. Not as though he was going to enjoy it, but as though it was something he was forced to do.

'Wait here,' he said and kissed her, hard and fierce, bruising her soft mouth with the desperation of his. Under his breath he pleaded, 'Trust me, Clary, *please*.'

Astonished, she watched his lithe figure leave the room. She was still standing in exactly the same position when he came back in through the door accompanied by a man who looked at her with her own eyes.

'Angus!' Very carefully she put her coffee cup down on a small marble table.

Angus was filled with a fierce exultation. He looked, she thought incredulously, as though he was enjoying himself. But as he saw her stricken face his own softened. 'Go away, love,' he ordered gruffly, his eyes already swinging back to the owner of this luxurious room.

It almost made her ill. Angus couldn't wait to sample the deadly fascination of measuring his strength with Morgan. The blood seemed to recede from her heart as she turned blindly towards the door.

'Stay right where you are,' Morgan said softly from across the room.

Brother and sister froze. Morgan smiled, his narrowed eyes fixed on Angus, but it was to Clary he spoke.

'Come here,' he commanded quite gently and held out his hand.

Clary stood motionless as her brother's face turned slowly towards her. She read his sudden bleak comprehension and searched for contempt, for hatred. He closed his eyes as if what he saw was unbearable, and she took a step towards him.

'Clary,' Morgan said softly.

Her eyes flicked from Angus, so dearly loved a brother, to Morgan, loved, hated, desired. She hesitated, bitterly angry with both of them. They were demanding that she make a choice, but each man knew that whatever her decision it would make her savagely unhappy.

She said, 'This has nothing to do with me, has it? I'm just the convenient focus.'

Both men broke off the silent, murderous confrontation to stare at her. She had never felt so alone, so friendless. She swallowed and continued harshly, 'It's Susan you're fighting over.'

Angus began to speak but she interrupted his first word, her eyes black with pain. 'You blame Morgan for stealing her from you. When I saw her in London she told me that he had no idea that she was married, not until after she'd left you. So you're blaming him because Susan wanted him. How many women have wanted you? Should you be blamed because they looked at you and decided that you'd probably be good in bed?'

The harsh planes and angles of Angus's face seemed to constrict as pain bit into his expression. He said nothing; he appeared to be looking at her and seeing something too horrible to credit.

'Do you want to punish Clary for Susan's decision to leave you?' Morgan's voice was level, almost indifferent, but Clary could see a tiny muscle in his jaw jerk. 'Do you despise your sister as well as your adulterous wife?'

Angus walked heavily across to the window and stood staring out. After a long, tense silence he said, 'If she is your mistress, yes.'

'And if she were my wife?'

Clary tasted the salt taste of her own blood and only then realised that she had bitten into her lip. She felt impotent, an onlooker watching two great beasts of prey, each intent on the slash across the jugular, the killing blow. They humiliated her with their casual arrogance, yet she could not intervene. She shivered on the brink of the enormous gulf that can stretch between male and female and realised that in a strange way they were ranged together against her.

'Why should I feel better about her being your wife?'

'Perhaps because it would mean that I love her.'

Almost conversationally Angus asked, 'And what would you do if someone stole her from you?'

Clary had thought no tension could be greater than that of the last few minutes, but she was mistaken. Morgan hesitated, his assurance tilting under the brutal honesty of the question. He did not look at Clary. He did not appear to look anywhere but inwards. Angus swung around, and she saw in him a threat and a promise, the full force of his will bent on the man he hated.

Holding her breath she waited, aware that he was forcing Morgan to face an issue he had not expected to have to confront.

At last he said without inflection, 'I don't believe that anything but death could take her from me. If that happened I would follow her. I have no interest in a world where she doesn't exist.'

But Angus was merciless. 'If she wanted to go, to walk out of that door and never come back. What then?'

Morgan was white beneath his tan and for the first time in ages he looked at Clary. She cried out at what she saw in his face. 'Then I'd have to let her go,' he said painfully, for once unable to conceal how difficult it was for him to accept the conclusion. 'Love is worth nothing unless it is freely given.'

Impossible not to believe him. Clary's breath came hissing between her teeth and Angus's big body seemed to relax. 'In that case,' he said, 'I withdraw my objection. But you'd better make her happy, or you will have me to answer to.'

'She is,' Morgan told him wryly as he held out his hand, 'quite capable of calling me to answer herself.'

Angus said nothing, but he shook Morgan's hand and came across to where Clary waited. He touched her cheek and said, 'Be happy, love.'

She strained up to kiss him; it was impossible to discern his emotions, but a familial instinct warned her that he was intensely unhappy.

He left them to a silence deeper and more profound than any before. Clary could not break it, she knew that Morgan had to be the one to speak. When he looked at her it was with chin held high as he hid any signs of the vulnerability Angus had forced him to reveal.

'So now you know,' he said.

Stumbling, her mouth dry, she ran to him, her arms encircling him in an embrace which was fierce and protective.

'I don't deserve that,' she whispered. 'I will never deserve that, but oh, I love you!'

'Do you, Clary?' His lean body relaxed; he lifted shaking hands to frame her face and tilted it to meet his tender gaze.

Shocked, she realised that he had not believed it, that he needed her reassurance.

'Can't you feel?' she asked huskily, guiding his hand to where her heart threatened to burst through the confines of her flesh.

But he resisted, imprisoning her in the cage of his arms.

'Not that,' he said almost bitterly. 'Oh, it's the most exquisite torment, but sex is not the most important part of our relationship. That first time I saw you, across the pony ring, I wanted to pick you up and carry you off and make love to you until I'd imprinted myself on every cell of your body, every thought process in your brain, made you completely dependent on me for happiness. Then you picked up the child and I thought you were married. I can't tell you what it was like. I felt as furious and vengeful as if I'd been betrayed. I was horrified to discover that I was coolly deciding on ways and means of breaking up the marriage.'

Clary's eyes widened in something very like the horror he had described as they searched the strained contours of his face.

'You might well be shocked,' he said half angrily. 'I shocked myself. I'd always been so determined not to get tangled up with married women ... I began to wonder if my moral standards had slipped ... I suppose I blamed you a little. Then Leona told me who you were, and I was—excited, as I'd never been before, like a youth when he realises this is it, he's about to have sex for the first time, he's going to crack the mystery of a woman's body.'

She tried to smile, awed by the strength of his emotion but hurting for him. 'I thought that it was the first car that gave rise to such anticipation.'

'That's a face-saver.' His hands moved, slid down to the slender curve of her shoulder, the fingers finding their way to the nape of her neck while his thumbs pushed her face up. 'That night showed me that although you were frightened and resentful you felt the same way, and I was gloating, I thought that from then on it would be easy. But everything went wrong. I was no longer in control. I didn't mean to ask you to go to London with me, but you got to me so hard that I blurted it out and you cut me down to size by reminding me of Susan.'

For a second every muscle in her body tensed. He gave a hard painful sigh and closed his eyes for a second. Clary's mouth shook.

He said heavily, 'My heart's love, if ever I was punished for my attitude to sex, that was it. What we

have is special, it was totally outside my experience
and I didn't know how to cope. I was afraid. I realised
that we both needed a breathing-space, time to come
to terms with the idea of love, even though the waiting
would be hell. I didn't sleep that night at Chase. I
walked the floor, alternately cursing my crassness and
making plans.'

'What plans?' she asked softly when the deep voice
hesitated.

'I decided to break with Susan, get her out of my
life, then go back to Chase to establish some sort of
basis for the future. I spent those weeks in a fever of
activity. I had business to deal with too. Anyway, I
thought in my arrogance that everything was going
along nicely. Then you saw me with Susan and the
world blew up in my face.'

Clary rested her proud head on his shoulder. His
mouth searched the soft curls to find her temple.
Through the silken tangle she could feel the heat in his
kiss and the way his lips trembled as though he was in
a fever. Suddenly protective, her arms tightened about
him.

'It just reinforced all I'd believed of you,' she said
into his neck. 'I thought that you were a rake, that you
didn't care, provided the woman was beautiful and
willing. You were so vivid, so blazing with life, and I
could see that every woman who saw you was
conscious of you. When I saw you and Susan together
I felt bereft, as though something beautiful had been
smirched. And I was furious. But beneath it all, I was
in despair because I knew there was no future for us. I
was bitterly, viciously jealous of Susan, and I told
myself that I hated you.'

'My God, that was obvious,' he muttered. 'You
looked magnificent, like an angry goddess. You
terrified Susan and you scared the hell out of me!'

She gave a throaty chuckle and touched the tip of
her tongue to the salty skin of his throat, relishing the

quick intake of his breath and the sudden clenching of his arms about her. 'It didn't show,' she said.

His amusement was self-derisory. 'I realised that if I betrayed any fear you'd have the whip hand, and that would mean finish.' In an urgent, almost pleading voice he said, 'I didn't touch her after I'd seen you. I couldn't. I took her with me that night because the arrangements had been made before my visit to Chase and I couldn't in all honour back out. For some reason she insisted on coming with me, even though she knew it was all over. By then I'd organised her enrolment at that college and put her into her flat.'

'You'd paid her off,' Clary said flatly.

'Yes.' He made no excuses.

Clary faced facts. What Morgan had done before she met him was no concern of hers. She had used his affair with Susan as a red herring to defend herself against the intense physical attraction and then the growing love she had felt for him. She could not agree with his attitude towards those affairs, but she was not naïve enough to believe that he had developed those attitudes without help. A man with his looks and sexuality must always have had women eager first to teach and then to sample his skills as a lover.

All that she had to ask herself now was whether he would remain faithful and with a shock of recognition she realised that she had never doubted his fidelity. It was as if that first bold, burning look had welded them together in a partnership which they both recognised, both accepted, a commitment in which there was no room for anyone else.

'I was afraid too,' she said slowly. 'I was a coward. I thought that emotions so fierce had to lead to pain.'

He lifted her chin and looked into her troubled eyes, his own very direct and loving. 'I knew what I was fighting. Angus and Susan were only your excuses. I had to convince you that you were safe with me, that I could not betray you the way your father and Angus were betrayed.'

She nodded, releasing the past with no regrets. 'I love you,' she said, her expression almost blinding in its joy, to be answered by an identical pulse of joy in his dark features.

'I adore you,' he muttered, punctuating the words with tiny kisses across her face. 'I worship you, I need you, I ache for you—I *love* you! And I'm so sorry you had to endure a scene like that with Angus, but it was the only way I could see to break the deadlock. He had to know that you would be happy with me, that you love me. I knew that once he realised how much you loved me he'd give in.'

'How did you know?'

His smile was tenderly mocking. 'Because, my lovely, he loves you. He realised that if he forced you to make a choice between him and me you'd be torn in two. I gambled on him not being able to do that, and you see, I was right.'

'You gambled on his affection for me being more powerful than his need for revenge?' she whispered, horrified.

'Yes. I followed a hunch—well, not that much of a risk. I gambled on that family loyalty you bristle with.' He laughed softly and kissed her wide eyes closed. 'I must say I admire him. He salved some pride by forcing that admission from me. Until I had to say it I hadn't really accepted how much I needed you, and loved you, and how afraid I was that my need, my love weren't going to be enough. He and I came out of that bout with honours about even.'

'He's never going to like you, is he?'

He responded to her sad question with the truth. 'No, I think he'll always hate my guts. He's a strong man and a hard one, but I'll always be thankful that he is an honest one. He realised that he couldn't take his revenge at the expense of your happiness. Perhaps if he falls in love again, the sting will go from his memories. And, of course, he'll see how very, very happy we are going to be . . .'

Clary nodded, intent for the moment on achieving some kind of balance between the joyful ecstasy of her love and the awakening passion which was beating up through her in slow, dark pulses.

'I'm so glad you love me,' she said dreamily, pressing slow warm kisses into his throat. 'I've been so miserable. If I'd known sooner——'

'You knew,' he said deeply, 'right from the start. You just wouldn't admit it, or accept it, not even after you seduced me with such delicious wantonness.'

Her skin prickled, first cold, then hot, at the laughter in his handsome pirate's face. 'You never actually said that you *loved* me,' she protested.

He held her away, compelling her to meet his regard. 'You knew,' he said implacably.

'I suppose I did.'

'I had to be sure,' he said, pulling her back into his arms. She shuddered as he ran his hand with leisurely precision down the length of her spine, urging her into the cradle of his hips so that his arousal became blatantly obvious. His mouth swooped, crushing hers beneath it.

Clary responded as she would always respond, accepting the swift brutality as a symbol of a need for reassurance which he would probably never express openly. He sighed, and the erotic punishment gentled.

'I was terrified this morning,' he astounded her by admitting raggedly. 'I thought I might have to prove to Angus just how much you loved me, and that would have humiliated you.'

She shivered, her quick mind supplying some of the methods he could have used to wring that proof from her. Now she knew him well enough to accept that he would have been merciless; his love was not weak or feeble. It could hurt, it could cut her to the bone, yet it was genuine emotion, not the violent lust she had once judged it to be. She lifted her eyes, meeting his with wry mockery, and saw the gold deep within flame up to hide the green. Beneath her hand his skin was heated and dry. She remembered the drawn, hungry contours which passion created in his face, and an answering flare of emotion lit the deep blue behind her lashes.

'He had to know,' he said silkily, 'that what you feel for me is stronger than any sisterly love, stronger than death, because that's the way I feel about you. I never thought it would happen to me, I was like you, scared of love. I saw what happened to my mother when my father died. That's why I handled it so badly.'

'Oh, I know,' she said almost inaudibly, kissing the crease in his cheek between each word. 'You don't— you *can't*—look at someone and fall fathoms deep in love, just like that!'

'Exactly.' He grinned wickedly. 'Perhaps we're the only two in the world to have done it.'

'Perhaps everyone in love believes that.'

'Ah, but we know it's true just for us.' He kissed her, kissed her again and then, with an effort of will which straightened the line of his mouth, put her away from him. 'Right, now we have to organise a wedding. I might just be able to keep my hands off you for the three days it will take——'

'You don't have to.'

He gave her a fierce, lancing glare. 'Don't have to what? Damn it, Clary, I want to marry you!'

She touched his mouth with a delicate probing forefinger. 'You don't have to wait, darling.'

His tongue curled around the fingertip. As she withdrew it he asked unevenly, 'Are you seducing me again?'

Strangely shy, her cheeks glowing with colour, she nodded.

'And you do it so well,' he said on an odd inflection. 'Do you mind if we wait until we're married?'

'No, of course not,' she said in a small voice.

He smiled very tenderly down at her. 'My heart's delight, this is new territory for me, a different country. Right from the start I knew that it wouldn't take much pressure from me to get you into bed, but I—oh, call it superstition, call it what you like—I was afraid I might lose you if I was too greedy, too hasty. I wanted your loving surrender, not your resentful compliance. As I told you, I wanted everything, and I was prepared to wait for it.'

Such iron self-control, she thought dazedly while her lips shaped words she barely heard. 'Then did I spoil everything that night by the pool?'

'No,' he whispered, sliding his arms about her as he collapsed slowly back on to the sofa.

When he lifted his head she was aching and clamorous with desire, and the colour ran dark along his suddenly prominent cheekbones. The pace of Clary's heart matched his, pounding so noisily that it was impossible to tell whose was loudest. He was tense with a feverish passion, fighting hard to regain that control she had thought unassailable.

'No,' he muttered, 'that was magical. You came up out of the water like an enchantress and my heart stopped. I felt like the shepherd when the moon goddess chose him for her lover, as if I'd been honoured above all men. And when we made love you were warm and erotic and ardent, generous and wildly passionate, and I lost my head, I had to lose myself in you even though it meant my plans went to hell.'

'What plans?' She spoke drowsily, fighting to control the hunger which could only be eased in the blind ecstasy of love.

'Oh, I wanted you on edge and eager, too frustrated to be able to deny me when we faced Angus.' His mouth twisted derisively before relaxing into soft laughter. 'But you came to me and you gave me all that I had ever wanted. I felt ten feet tall because your surrender meant that I had you, mine for all time. Angus was easy to deal with after that.'

She nodded. 'I love you.'

He touched his lips to her forehead, to her dazzled eyes, then to the freckles across her nose, finally, tormentingly, to the cleft in her chin. 'And I love you,' he murmured. 'It's a very willing surrender, my dearest love.'

She turned her face into the warmth and security of him, happy as she had never been before in her life, lulled by this tenderness she had not expected in him. 'Oh, a *very* willing surrender. For all time.'

There would be times of tribulation ahead, but this complete confidence in each other's love, this was for ever. Smiling, Clary reached for him and relinquished the last fear and let it drift away.

Harlequin Presents

Coming Next Month

983 STANDING ON THE OUTSIDE Lindsay Armstrong
An Australian secretary is drawn out when her new boss goes out of his way to make her smile...enjoy life again. But what's the point if his heart still belongs to his childhood sweetheart?

984 DON'T ASK ME NOW Emma Darcy
How can a country girl from Armidale trust her heart to her uppercrust business partner? Especially when his attraction coincides with the renewed interest of the first man to reject her as not being good enough to marry.

985 ALL MY TOMORROWS Rosemary Hammond
In war-torn San Cristobal a nurse falls hard for an injured reporter, who then disappears from her life. She knows she must forget him. But how can she, when he finds her again in her home town.

986 FASCINATION Patricia Lake
Emotionally scarred by the last suitor shoved her way, a young American finds a merchant banker difficult to trust—particularly when their bedside wedding in her grandfather's hospital room is arranged by her grandfather and the groom!

987 LOVE IN THE DARK Charlotte Lamb
The barrister an Englishwoman once loved threatens to revive the scandal that drove them apart five years ago—unless she breaks off with her fiancé and marries him instead.

988 A GAME OF DECEIT Sandra Marton
A magazine reporter, traveling incognito, wangles an invitation to stay at a famous actor's private hideaway in the Mexican Sierra Madre. But she's the one who begins to feel vulnerable, afraid of being exposed.

989 VELVET PROMISE Carole Mortimer
A young divorcée returns to Jersey and falls in love with her ex-husband's cousin. But he still thinks she married for money. If only she could tell him how horribly wrong he is!

990 BITTERSWEET MARRIAGE Jeneth Murrey
Turndowns confuse a job-hunting woman until she discovers the souce of her bad luck—the powerful English businessman she once walked out on. Finally he's in a position to marry her!

Available in June wherever paperback books are sold, or through Harlequin Reader Service:

In the U.S.
901 Fuhrmann Blvd.
P.O. Box 1397
Buffalo, N.Y. 14240-1397

In Canada
P.O. Box 603
Fort Erie, Ontario
L2A 5X3

Take 4 books & a surprise gift FREE

SPECIAL LIMITED-TIME OFFER

Mail to   **Harlequin Reader Service®**

In the U.S.   In Canada
901 Fuhrmann Blvd.   P.O. Box 609
P.O. Box 1394   Fort Erie, Ontario
Buffalo, N.Y. 14240-1394   L2A 5X3

YES!   Please send me 4 free Harlequin Romance® novels and my free surprise gift. Then send me 6 brand-new novels every month as they come off the presses. Bill me at the low price of $1.66 each*—a 15% saving off the retail price. There are no shipping, handling or other hidden costs. There is no minimum number of books I must purchase. I can always return a shipment and cancel at any time. Even if I never buy another book from Harlequin, the 4 free novels and the surprise gift are mine to keep forever.   116 BPR BP7S

*$1.75 in Canada plus 69¢ postage and handling per shipment.

Name	(PLEASE PRINT)	
Address		Apt. No.
City	State/Prov.	Zip/Postal Code

This offer is limited to one order per household and not valid to present subscribers. Price is subject to change.   DOR-SUB-1A

Janet Dailey

Americana

A romantic tour of America with
Janet Dailey!

Enjoy two releases each month from this
collection of your favorite previously
published Janet Dailey titles, presented
alphabetically state by state.

Available NOW wherever paperback books
are sold.

GILLIAN HALL

The magnificent novel of a woman fighting for her greatest passion— and for a love to fulfill her deepest desires.

The desire to break from an unbearable past takes prima ballerina Anna Duras to Broadway, in search of the happiness she once knew. The tumultuous changes that follow lead her to the triumph of new success . . . and the promise of her greatest love.

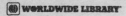